girl with GUITAR

girl with GUITAR

a novel

This book is a work of fiction. The names, characters, places, and incidents are products of the author's imagination or have been used fictitiously and are not to be construed as real. Any resemblance to persons, living or dead, actual events, locale or organizations is entirely coincidental.

First paperback edition May 2013
Cover Design by Emily Mah Tippetts
www.emtippetts.com
Editor: Mickey Reed
Manufactured in the United States of America
ISBN-13: 978-1484835265
ISBN-10: 1484835263

For H.G.S.

Never be afraid to follow your dreams. And your heart.

In Loving Memory

Nikkole Lynn Hapner

11.13.81 - 03.16.12

I know you're listening to our favorite songs in Heaven. The soundtrack of our many crazy adventures is the one that will never stop playing in my head. Until we meet again my sweet friend. Put on some Lynyrd Skynyrd when you see me coming.

"Hi, Daddy." Kylie's usually clear voice was soft and thick with emotion. At eighteen, she knew she sounded more like an eight-year-old when she spoke to him.

"Darla finally kicked me out…another one of her *friends* paid too much attention to me." She rolled her eyes, and heavy wet tears slid out. She wiped her face with the back of her hand while cussing herself for crying.

"Don't know why she wastes her time on any of them. None of them could ever compare to you." She huffed out a laugh over the dull pain in her chest. "I should probably write a song about it, huh?" She had big news, so she rushed on. "Speaking of songs, I'm going to Nashville like we talked about." Even though no one else was around, she lowered her voice to a whisper. "I'm going to make you proud, I promise."

After taking a few breaths and waiting for her tears to cease, she leaned closer, tracing the letters of their last name on the temporary marker. "Soon you'll have a real one, I swear. I don't care what I have to do. We'll get one of those fancy marble ones, like Mama has. Maybe get a guitar engraved on it. Would you like that?" Sobs racked her shoulders, familiar tremors accompanied by a hollow ache pulling her inward when he didn't answer.

There was more, so much more she wanted to say. So many things she should've said before it was too late. But just like in her nightmares, the ones where she was getting ready to go on stage and couldn't remember the lyrics to any of her songs, her throat tightened. Trapping the words within below the painful lump rising above. A horn sounded in the distance.

Her cab was waiting. It was time to go. So she said the one thing she wished she had the last time she saw him.

"Goodbye, Daddy."

chapter ONE

Oklahoma was a lot prettier when it was blurring out of sight. Even if it was hazy from the tears clouding her vision. The Greyhound jarred Kylie and her belongings. The ride was rough and smelled of gasoline, but she felt better than she had in months. She should've said goodbye to her best friend, Lulu, but she knew she'd just talk her out of it.

She'd visited her dad's grave and said her goodbyes, praying he'd understand.

After going by the house and seeing that Darla wasn't home, she'd used her key one last time. Kylie found her old pink suitcase, the one she'd used when visiting her grandmother before she'd passed. Once she'd crammed everything she could into it, she grabbed a banana and a Coke and called a cab to take her to the bus station.

She was $100 richer than she'd planned since her former boss, Ms. Pam, had felt guilty about letting her go and been generous. Kylie knew the money had probably come out of the old woman's own pocket. The cab ride to Oklahoma City had taken most of it.

Kylie clutched her guitar case and stared at her nearly transparent reflection in the window. A few lyrics floated through her mind about holding what you have as you let go of what you've lost, but she didn't have the energy to write them down. It was a thirteen-hour bus ride that cost her a hundred and fifty bucks, but it was worth it.

THREE filthy gas station bathrooms later, Kylie found herself in the heart of Nashville. It was even more amazing than she'd imagined, but the bus ride had pretty much sucked all of the hope right out of her.

She got out her cell phone and pulled up the app to find the nearest hotel. There was an Extended Stay Nashville near Printer's Alley that only ran about sixty bucks a night. It was do-able. Maybe not for long, but all she needed was something to focus on right now.

Anything to keep her mind off the fact that she might've just made the biggest mistake of her life.

After checking in and showering, she broke down and called her best friend. When she told her where she was, Lulu's reaction was pretty much what she expected.

"Have you lost your ever-loving mind?" *Yes.*

"I know it sounds crazy Lu, but—"

"Sounds crazy? No, it is freaking crazy. Kylie, you're all alone in a city you've never been to before where you don't know anyone. What if something happens to you? What the hell were you thinking?"

"Please listen."

"Listening." Lulu sighed her impatience through the phone. She sounded a lot closer than she actually was.

Kylie took a deep breath and tried to explain her temporary insanity. "I lost my dad, Darla kicked me out after she walked in on what she thought was another one of her skeezy boyfriends trying to make a move, and then I went to work and got fired. Don't take this the wrong way, Lu, but when you bailed on our Nashville trip this summer, I felt like I was about to lose my dream, too. There's nothing for me in Pride, Oklahoma. And please do not guilt trip me because, as long as I can afford to keep my phone on, we can talk every day. I swear."

"You know I couldn't go to Nashville because I have to visit my dad in California. It wasn't like I didn't want to go with you. But he rearranged his whole schedule and it's been so long since—"

"I get it, I do. Trust me. If I could have one day back with my dad, there's not much I wouldn't trade to get it. It's just…it was time. I can't explain it, but this is where I'm meant to be." Kylie had cut her friend off because she did understand, completely. If she could have one more day with her dad, she'd pick that over watching her friend choke at open mic night any day.

Her best friend let out an exaggerated huff that sounded almost like understanding. Lulu's voice was softer when she spoke again. "Soo…the stepmonster's boy toy. Anything really happen?"

Kylie laughed. "That is what you'd be thinking about. Sorry, but no. It was totally innocent. Awkward as hell, but innocent. I spilled my Coke on my work shirt and he was in the middle of loaning me one to replace it. Darla just walked in at the wrong moment and freaked. Pretty sure she's been looking for an excuse to get rid of me for a while now."

After Kylie's dad had been killed in a freak accident at the factory where he worked, his widow, the thirty-five-year-old former beauty queen, had made it pretty clear she wasn't interested in letting Kylie continue to live in the house she'd grown up in.

"So like, what are you going to do there?" Lulu sounded more concerned than judgmental. Kylie could practically see her friend's brow wrinkling as she twirled a lock of her hair, whatever color it was today.

"Um, I just checked into a hotel that I should be able to afford for at least a week. I'm going to get up early tomorrow and walk Music Row and Printer's Alley looking for bars and diners that might be hiring."

"Okay, then what?"

"Then I'm going to put an ad in the paper. 'Girl with guitar, needs money to record demo, will do anything.'" Kylie laughed but she could hear her best friend mumbling obscenities. "I'm kidding, Lu. I'm going to sign up for every amateur night I can get on the list for and save my pennies until I can record a demo. Then I'll send it out and pray."

She was already scheduled to perform at The Rum Room's upcoming open mic night. They'd had an all call on a website that Kylie had come across and she'd signed up months ago. It was the reason for the trip she and her best friend had planned…and canceled.

"I'll pray too," her best friend whispered. Kylie suspected from the sniffles she heard that she might be crying.

"How are the twins?" Lulu's six-year-old brothers usually served as a topic for lighter conversation. Since her mom worked two jobs, Lulu was pretty much raising them while attending beauty school in Owasso part-time. When they first started talking, both boys had pronounced Olivia as Lulu, and the nickname had stuck. Kylie couldn't even imagine calling her friend anything else.

"They're good. Rotten as usual, and Lord help me if I find one more lizard or slimy-ass frog they've brought in this trailer…"

Kylie giggled, though she couldn't help the twinge of envy she felt towards her friend for having a family. People to eat meals with, talk to, laugh with, argue with. She'd lost all of that when her dad died.

"Love you, Lu. I'm going to be okay, I promise," Kylie said, because she was too tired to keep talking. She hoped this didn't count as a lie since she at least hoped it was true.

chapter TWO

A FEW bucks short of a hundred dollars to her name, Kylie was ready to give up on whatever crazy-ass dream she'd chased to Nashville. Nearly two weeks at the hotel, plus food, and still no job had left her with next to nothing.

After the fourth rejection that Saturday, she trudged around town aimlessly. Everywhere she'd gone had a waiting list a mile long. For waitresses. Many of which were aspiring singers and songwriters. So much for being original. Nearly a year of saving money to buy her father a headstone, and it was gone in two weeks. Only two places had even taken her resume after she filled out an application. A restaurant called the Back Alley Diner and a bar slash nightclub called Whiskey Jack's. Neither had called. In fact, no one had called.

A red guitar's bright neon lights flickered to life as Kylie passed underneath. Somehow she'd wandered to The Rum Room. The Amateur Night she was signed up for at this exact bar was still two weeks away, and the way things were going she might be homeless by then. Darla had gotten her dad's '88 Chevy pickup when he died so Kylie wouldn't even have that to sleep in when she ran out of hotel money. She'd already filled out an application to waitress at The Rum Room, but she sulked in anyways, figuring there would at least be some decent music to listen to on a Saturday night.

A bluesy band with a jazzy twang was on stage when Kylie entered. She paid the six dollar cover, knowing good and well that it would cost her a meal. But the more she heard of the band, the more she was convinced it was worth it.

Kylie lowered herself into a seat near the bar and listened with her entire body. Within minutes her boot was tapping along with the bass and her body swayed with the singer's soothing voice. Yeah, this was definitely better than food any day.

"What can I getcha, darlin'?" a brunette waitress with hair teased to Jesus asked. She reminded Kylie of a younger Ms. Pam, her boss back in Oklahoma, but with more eye shadow and a better body.

"Um, I'm really just here to see the band," Kylie answered, knowing she didn't need to waste another three bucks on a Coke.

"Got it. Enjoy." The waitress winked and spun over to another table.

Kylie knew that look. The woman had thought she was a fangirl groupie. She surveyed the crowd and it was mostly young and female. Ah. Usually she found those girls shallow and annoying for the most part, but at that particular moment the lead singer was looking pretty hot. Though it didn't seem to be him everyone was here to see. Most of the other clientele were busy texting and paying more attention to each other than the band.

"Damn it, where the hell is he?" Two men stood between Kylie's seat and the bar. They didn't seem too happy to see each other.

"He'll be here, Clive. The bus got stuck in traffic," a handsome gray-haired man with a goatee promised a heavy set man who wore rings on nearly every finger.

"This is the third time, Pauly. I don't give a damn who he is, he's taking up valuable slots and pissing people off. Most importantly, *me*."

"Um, Clive?" Kylie's waitress looked less than enthusiastic about interrupting the two men.

"Yeah?" the man who must have been Clive responded, glaring at her as if she were responsible for all the world's problems. Kylie knew it was impolite to stare but she felt a little scared for the waitress who'd been so nice to her before.

"Kimmie's not coming. She got an offer to play at some big time party so she won't be making her shift."

"You gotta be kidding me." Clive dragged a thick hand over his face. "Tell her she's fired."

"Um, seriously? Clive we're shorthanded as it is and who else is going to handle hospitality and the green room?" The waitress shifted her tray to the other arm.

"I'm looking at her, unless you want to collect your last check the same day Kimmie does." The large man glared at the brunette until she nodded and backed away. Once she was gone he went back to arguing with Pauly.

Kylie said a quick prayer and held her breath. "Hey, um, ma'am?" she called out, flagging down the waitress.

"Yeah, sugar. You change your mind?" The woman sat her tray on Kylie's table and pulled out her order pad.

"Um, oh, uh no."

The weary-looking woman lowered her tablet. "Then what can I do for you?"

Kylie could tell she was starting to get pissed. "I'm a waitress. I mean, I have waitressing experience and good references and—"

"Can you start right now?"

Kylie's heart leapt into her throat. "Yeah! I mean, yes ma'am."

"How old are you?" The woman eyed her up and down.

"Eighteen." She almost added that she'd be nineteen in two months, but that sounded like something a little kid would say.

"Okay, listen close because I'm only going to say this once. You are my cousin who just moved here from…hell, where are you from?"

"Oklahoma."

"Perfect. I'm Tonya by the way."

"Nice to meet you, cuz." Kylie grinned.

Tonya just rolled her eyes. "Let's go, kid."

After a gruff introduction to Clive himself, who apparently owned the place, Tonya tossed Kylie a menu and an apron and told her she was hired.

An hour in, Kylie knew this was nothing like Pam's Country Kitchen, the homestyle buffet she'd worked at back home, and that she'd just gotten in way over her head. Though the tips were much better. Three hours in, the band that was supposed to show still hadn't and Clive was livid. Kylie had been pinched and patted in places she didn't even want to think about by customers she could barely see in the dimly lit bar. But no way in hell was she going to mention that to Clive.

Her back ached, her feet were numb, and her head pounded. When

Clive passed by and asked how it was going, she smiled broadly and said, "Fantastic!" with all the enthusiasm she could muster. He grunted something that seemed remotely like approval and moved on. When Tonya said it was break time, Kylie nearly collapsed into the nearest chair.

Tonya grabbed her by the shoulder and hauled her right back up. "Oh no, cuz. Got something to show you." The waitress led Kylie past the stage and down a hallway that she hadn't even noticed before.

"Hospitality room for media." Tonya rapped on a door to her left just as she pushed it open. The plush room was mostly beige with some wooden accents. A couch that probably cost as much as Kylie's house back home sat up against a wall. A small dark table with two wooden chairs sat next to it. A long buffet table held the remnants of what looked like a pretty impressive dinner buffet. Picked-over portions of barbecued chicken, pasta salad, a fruit tray, and a few rolls remained.

Kylie's stomach growled at the sight. She'd been living on stale pizza for nearly two weeks.

"You hungry?" Tonya had obviously noticed Kylie's mouth watering.

"A little," she said, sure she was turning red with embarrassment.

"Well, help yourself. Eat while we walk."

Kylie scooped up a piece of chicken, stuffed it into a roll, and followed Tonya out the door.

"Okay so, hospitality room for media is cake compared to the green room," she said as she opened the door at the end of the hall.

Kylie nearly choked on her sandwich. This room alone was nicer than the bar itself. A leather sectional sat across from a flat screen television that took up most of the wall. A large oak table contained trays filled with chicken wings, sliders, and potato skins covered in cheese. Bottles of beer and water sat next to the spread. Kylie snagged a bottle of water on her way past.

Beyond that was a small but nice kitchen with a stainless steel fridge and microwave. A pool table and mini bar were tucked behind the kitchen. Around the corner was a bathroom complete with a shower stall.

"This room is nicer than where I'm staying," she told Tonya.

"Yeah, it's nicer than my apartment, too, and a hell of a lot harder to clean."

"It's my job to clean it, isn't it?" Kylie asked as reality set it. *Okay, no problem*, she thought to herself. A dream come true had to come with a downside.

"Yeah." Tonya smiled with sympathy in her eyes. "But we'll tag team it till you get the hang of it."

"Thanks." Kylie didn't know if this woman was an angel or just a decent human being, but she really wanted to hug her. She resisted, but just barely. "So um, how much…I just mean, not that it's a big deal or anything." Kylie stuttered over the embarrassing question.

"Enough," Tonya answered with a wink. "Just be sure you tip out the bartender every night and all will be well."

Kylie had done that with the hostesses at Pam's. But only like five percent. "How much do you tip out?"

"Twenty percent is standard, thirty if you want to get your drinks to your customers before they grow old. Tips will be shitty tonight 'cause some hotshot singer was a no-show, but most nights it's pretty good."

"Got it. Anything else I should know?"

"Yeah, until Clive puts you on the schedule, you're just auditioning and this isn't Oklahoma, honey. You were in the right place at the right time and I appreciate it, believe me." Tonya cocked one hip and placed a hand on it. When she spoke again, her voice was softer. "I have a two-year-old home with a babysitter, and if you hadn't come along I'd be cleaning these rooms until three in the morning. But Clive…he's, well, he's a hard ass." Kylie watched the woman shrug. "We open at two every afternoon. It's appetizers only until four when they fire up the grill. Most acts go on at seven. We're supposed to kick everyone out at midnight but most nights regulars stay till two. Sometimes the bands don't leave until then and we can't clean the rooms until they're gone."

Her brain was working overtime to retain the information the woman was hurling at her. Basically she'd be working two in the afternoon until two in the morning. Should be a hell of a paycheck. The thought of an apartment of her very own appeared in the back of her mind.

The waitress studied her for a second and then sighed. "Listen, if it's too much, just finish out tonight and don't come back. No hard feelings, I swear—this ain't for everyone."

Kylie shook her head. "No, I'm good. Promise."

"Okay well, until he puts you on that schedule," Tonya began, gesturing to a giant dry erase board just outside of a door she said led to Clive's office, "you show up at one. Every day."

"Got it."

"And Kylie?" Tonya stopped and turned so abruptly they almost collided.

"Yeah?"

"Boots and jeans are good, but tomorrow wear a tighter t-shirt."

Kylie swallowed any worries this should cause. "Hey Tonya," she said as she followed her back into the bar.

"Yeah?"

"Thanks…I mean it."

"For what?" the brunette asked with an arched brow.

"Being the best cousin ever."

Tonya laughed out loud. It was the first time Kylie had seen her do so. She looked ten years younger. "Kid, you're either crazy or desperate—and you have to be both to make it here. I think you're gonna do just fine."

Both, Kylie thought to herself. *I'm both.*

chapter THREE

AFTER showing up at twelve-thirty every day for two weeks, Clive stopped ignoring her. She'd worn the tightest shirts she owned. She'd even tied some up in the back because hey, a girl's gotta eat.

"Well, I guess you're not going back to Idaho, huh?" the bar owner asked, clapping a big hand on Kylie's shoulder. She briefly debated correcting him but thought better of it.

"No, sir. I'm afraid you're stuck with me," she told him, shifting the enormous tray of wings and beer she was carrying to the arm he wasn't clamped onto.

"All right. Next week you'll be on the schedule. Good work, kid." He cleared his throat, and looked as if he was debating on whether or not to waste anymore time speaking to a random waitress. "I'm not easily impressed, but the hospitality rooms are lookin' better than ever and Tonya says you're a huge help. I got guys in the kitchen whose lives I've threatened if they try to ask you out and run you off." He winked at her and she grinned up at him.

"Thank you, um, for all of that." She was surprised to see his cold dark eyes warm for a second. There was a flash of something fatherly about him that set off a deep ache inside of her.

"Well get back to work before you make a liar out of me," he huffed, releasing her. *Back to business as usual,* Kylie thought. "Oh, and get with Tonya and fill out your W9, make a copy of your license and all that."

"Yes, sir." No more getting paid out of the cash register at the bar each night. Actual paychecks were coming soon. A daring sliver of hope settled in, causing her to grin like a crazy fool for the rest of her shift.

BETWEEN waitressing and setting up and cleaning the hospitality rooms, Kylie was exhausted. In the past two weeks she'd checked in with Lulu a few times, but mostly she just showered and wrote and worked out new songs with her guitar until she passed out cuddled up next to it each night.

Stumbling through her morning routine of showering and getting ready while contemplating splurging on expensive coffee, she was half dressed when she remembered it was Amateur Night. At The Rum Room. Where she worked.

She'd been so grateful for the tips that were keeping her housed and fed for the time being, she'd lost track of what day it was. How would Clive feel about this? And Tonya? Oh hell, it was entirely possible that there might be a rule banning employees from performing at these types of things.

On her brisk walk to work, guitar case thumping behind her, Kylie tried to think of how to pose the question to Tonya. If there was a rule, she knew she should probably keep her job and sign up for open mic nights at other bars. No shortage of those. But damn. She'd already seen the list of managers and music execs that frequented The Rum Room's Amateur Night. Not to mention the number of artists that had been discovered there. Talk about a blessing and a curse. It was everything she could do not to groan out loud.

When she arrived at work, she heard voices coming from the kitchen so she skirted the bar and slunk into the employee lounge. The hum of the Coke machine was the only sound she heard as she tucked her guitar behind the couch. She'd practiced for hours last night, and she knew exactly what song she would perform. *Goodbye Pride*, the new one. It was her song, her town, and the place where her father would remain buried forever.

Please God, do not let Clive fire me over this.

KYLIE had tried twice already to pull Tonya aside, but the bar was packed. She wasn't able to get her attention until almost seven, when open mic night would begin.

"Hey, cuz, I need to ask you about something, like *now*," Kylie whispered to her when they passed each other filling drink orders.

Tonya unloaded the empty glasses from her tray, replacing them with full ones. "Um, kinda busy here."

"I know, me too, but it's an emergency. Please, pretty please meet me in the lounge in five?"

"Okay, but this better be good." Tonya rolled her eyes and practically sprinted away to deliver her drinks.

A few minutes later, Tonya found Kylie warming up on her guitar in the employee lounge.

The waitress wiped her hands on her apron and folded her arms across her chest. "Really? Busiest night all week and you need me to listen to you play the guitar?"

Biting her lip so hard she almost drew blood, she took a deep breath and confessed. "I'm signed up for tonight. Think Clive will be pissed?"

Tonya sighed and dropped onto the couch beside her. "Well yeah, but only because the last girl who quit did the same thing. Met some big deal manager and is now on a hotel tour or something."

"But there's no rule against it, right?"

"No, there's not."

Unable to keep the grin off of her face, Kylie let loose a riff on her guitar. "Thank you, Jesus!"

"Well, I got Demonic Deb to watch my tables. She's probably stealing my tips as we speak, so let's hear something."

"Really?" Kylie could feel her soul lighting up.

"Yeah, and hurry. We gotta get back out there."

Kylie took a deep breath and launched into her song. *"Goodbye pride, it's time I let you go. It's hard to watch the place I love fade away, while holding on to what I know. But second chances and could've beens and things we should've said keep haunting me. Like ghosts of dreams passed with a grudge to hold, they just won't let it be. It's not like me to run away, to give up, or just leave town, but if I stay another day, this pride's gonna drag me down."* Kylie let the last chord hang in the air before picking up the tempo.

"Everybody's got a story to tell, a friendly sin that they know real well. I ain't ashamed to say that pride's mine. Because the last time was the last time." Swallowing hard to push down the emotions her lyrics stirred, Kylie closed her eyes and kept singing.

"So goodbye pride, it's time I let you go. Gonna let 'em say what they're gonna say, 'cause I'm the only one who knows. Pride's a cheap shot in a tall glass, and if you drink it slow you think it's gonna last, but I know better than that."

Even caught up in her music, she knew she was probably singing loud enough to be heard in the hall, so she lowered her voice. *"Everybody's got a story to tell. A love affair with a sin that they know real well, but pride's not gonna be mine. The last time was the last time. This time I'm letting you go. This is the end of what could've been. Now I guess we'll never know..."*

She cut the song off before the last chorus and opened her eyes. "Well?" she asked, looking up at Tonya. Who had tears in her eyes. "Whoa, hey, what's wrong?"

"That was beautiful, really. It was like you knew my whole life story, which you don't, thank God."

"Thanks." Kylie beamed.

"But you can't play that tonight," Tonya said evenly, dabbing her tears away with a bar napkin.

Her heart sank into her stomach. "I can't?"

"No." Kylie watched Tonya's eyes harden as she gripped her shoulder. "Listen to me, kid. I know a few things. Like for one, your life's goal is probably not to be a waitress in a honky tonk. And for two, I know that all you really want is to make it big in country music like every other kid in this town, and that's all fine and good and I'll say I knew you when. Matter of fact, hold up, sign this napkin."

Kylie's mouth gaped open at her friend's blunt observations. And she was seriously holding out a napkin and a pen. Slowly, Kylie took it and scribbled her name across it.

"But here's what else I know. If you go play that sappy song that no one knows the words to, everyone will smile and nod and keep right on drinking. The managers and talent scouts that show will keep texting on their phones and someone somewhere might say, 'That was a nice song,' or 'She was cute,' and that will be it."

"Okay, so..." Kylie was still too stunned to say much of anything. Tears threatened behind her eyes. This was the song she'd worked so hard on, put so much of herself into. Wasn't it a good thing to be original?

"So you get your cute little butt out there, you sing some Taylor Swift or Kelly whoever cover, and you shake it up and make it your own so the audience can sing along while not comparing you to whoever really sings the damn thing."

"Oh, is that all? Well, that should be a piece of cake. Thanks for the advice." Kylie rolled her eyes and left them focused on the ceiling so her tears wouldn't fall.

"Look, you can sing, you play good enough. You're kinda sexy and all that stuff they want. I wouldn't waste my breath or my time, Kylie, if you didn't just blow me the hell away, but I know this town. If this was your first day of meeting with a label exec, I'd say bust that song out. But this is a bar, and you need to get their attention first. The guys who come in here are looking for one thing. Acts that bring in money. People want to hear that song that makes them stand up and sing along and stay up drinking and partying all night. Think you can do that?"

Kylie swallowed hard, pushed her tears back behind her eyes, and forced a smile. She'd grown up without a mother. Buried the only man she'd ever loved less than a year ago. Lost everything in the blink of an eye. Surely she could do this. "Yeah. Yeah I can."

"Good, 'cause no matter what they call it, this shit ain't for amateurs." Tonya stood, offering her a weak smile before leaving Kylie all alone to figure out what the hell she was going to do.

chapter FOUR

GODSEND that she was, Tonya took over Kylie's tables while she warmed up in the lounge. Kylie ran to grab a bottle of water from the media room and bumped into a man she didn't recognize.

"God, sorry," she told him.

"Women usually don't call me that when I have all my clothes on."

Kylie arched an eyebrow and started to back out of the room with her water. *No time for douchebaggery tonight, buddy*. Tonya had warned her about slick looking guys who went around propositioning desperate waitresses in hopes of getting them naked in front of a camera.

"Hey, I was kidding," he said with a teasing grin. "Sort of. Michael Miller," he informed her, reaching out a hand.

Kylie eyed it as if it were a poisonous snake and he let it drop.

"And your name?" he inquired, dark eyes sparkling with amusement.

"Just a waitress. Excuse me." Kylie bolted from the room. She'd heard Clive welcoming everyone and knew she was third on the list to perform. She wondered if he'd seen her name on it yet.

Kylie darted to the employee bathroom and tried to freshen up. She wouldn't have time to change clothes so she'd worn her best jeans and the black Rum Room t-shirt Clive had just given her. After splashing water on her face, followed by some mascara and lip gloss, she exited into the hall to chug her bottle of water and wait in line with the other performers.

Leaning against the cool concrete wall, Kylie's stomach clenched and sweat dripped down her back. Several of the male amateurs waiting to perform gave her appraising glances but she was too nervous to care. Or talk. The few other girls in line looked like a cross between Hollywood hookers and country Barbie. One lady looked old enough to be her grandmother. *Dear God, please do not let me still be doing this at her age.*

No, she thought, *shame on me. Good for her for not giving up on her dream.* The possibility of homelessness and starvation had almost been enough to do her in.

The act just before her went on and her ears filled with rushing fluid and a faraway ringing. She prayed that Tonya was right and that what she was about to do would work. She'd gotten a good look at the crowd—mostly early to mid-twenties and the few usual old timers.

She wasn't at all sure that this was a good idea, but they definitely wouldn't be able to sit there and ignore her like they might have if she'd gone with her original plan. If this worked, and she made it anywhere in music, Kylie was going to send Tonya's kid to college.

"Next up! Well I'll be, if it isn't The Rum Room's very own Kylie Ryans, ladies and gentlemen." Nate, one of the short order cooks, introduced her and then stepped aside.

Kylie stepped onto the stage, ignoring the blinding lights, and walked over to talk to the drummer in the house band. She whispered in his ear and he nodded. She leaned over to the lead guitar player and said, "Watch me for changes." He gave her a thumbs up and waited. Here went nothing.

"Evenin' y'all," Kylie drawled into the microphone. "I had a song I was gonna sing and then my friend Tonya, she might be your waitress, she told me it sucked—so I guess I'm just gonna play this here guitar and see where it takes us." She grinned at the audience and then leaned closer to the mic once more. "Oh, and I go right back to serving after this, so if you don't clap when I'm finished, I can't be held responsible for what might happen to your drink between the bar and your table." Kylie winked and strummed a few cords. "Okay, here we go."

Laughter? Did she hear laughter? She thought she did.

I know you wanna tie me down, know you wanna put a ring on it, but I ain't never been that kinda girl, not for all the money in the world.

Kylie launched into her modified version of Trace Corbin's latest hit,

Not That Kinda Man. It was the famous bachelor's latest lovin' and leavin' single and she was attempting to turn the thing on its ear. He'd written and sang it as a sad break up ballad and Kylie had remixed and reworked it into the single girl's party anthem.

You wanna own me but you don't know me. Guess what darlin'? When you wake up I'll be gone.

Kylie flashed her sexiest grin and wiggled a little at the crowd. Then she shouted, "Sing it with me girls!" into the mic and picked up the tempo, launching into the chorus.

Several waitresses, Tonya included, stopped what they were doing to sing along. Not that Kylie could really see them, but the girls in the crowd joined in too. She sang to the guitar player, whose name she was pretty sure was Andy, and he played right along, smiling and winking at her the whole time. *Well I'm not that kinda girl, don't wanna play these games, not gonna wake up in your bed or take your name.* She gave Andy a playful smack on the ass and he blew her a kiss. Shrieking whistles radiated from the audience.

The music hummed and pulsed against her and somewhere in Kylie's mind a little voice said, *Holy shit you're doing it!*

When the number was over, she practically flew off the stage, painfully aware of the pounding in her chest. *Oh well, if I have a heart attack and die right this moment, I'll die happy.* The applause was loud enough to be heard over the ringing in her ears and she wanted it more than oxygen.

Clive was leaning on the bar, shaking his head but smiling. Tonya shot her two thumbs up. Kylie let out a little squeal of happiness and sent a silent thank you up to her daddy, feeling certain she was higher than any drug could ever take her.

She would let Tonya go home early tonight and do the rooms herself. She had enough energy to clean ten green rooms. When she told Tonya that, the woman hugged her. Hard. "You knocked 'em dead, girl! That was amazing!"

"Yeah, well, I got some really good advice," Kylie told her, unable to keep the permagrin off her face.

The next act stepped out of the shadows and took the stage. Kylie heard a deep male voice with a sexy southern drawl say, "Damn. Just my luck to have to follow that."

The audience was still shrieking and screaming and Kylie knew she'd done well, but seriously?

"I apologize for standing y'all up a few weeks ago. Musta got my dates mixed up. Probably time to fire that manager of mine," the handsome man on stage drawled.

Who was this guy? Whoever he was, the women in the audience were going crazy over him.

"Well, since that good looking waitress stole my number, guess I'll have to sing something else. Where is that girl anyways?"

Oh God. Oh God, *please no.* Kylie's heart sank and her high evaporated instantly. She turned to face the man on stage. Trace freaking Corbin was standing there with a guitar in one hand and the other to his eyes, scanning the crowd for...her.

chapter FIVE

There was only one way out of this. Okay, maybe two. Duck and hide and risk losing her job, or face the man whose song she'd just butchered in front of several hundred people. And risk losing her job.

Well, she'd never been one to back down, and she'd never ducked and hid from anyone in her life. Certainly not some cocky-ass country music singer who everyone knew was pretty much drinking his career down the drain.

"Can I get you a drink, Mr. Corbin?" Kylie asked in the sweetest tone she could muster, stepping towards the stage.

"No, ma'am. Got one," he told her, winking at the audience and lifting a beer bottle in her direction. Thick dark hair peeked out from under a trucker's hat, and muscular suntanned forearms flexed at the end of his rolled up shirtsleeves. His bright white smile was framed by boyish dimples, and damn those jeans were doing things to her.

"Then what can I do for you?" she asked, rolling her eyes at the crowd as if she was annoyed with the megastar for interrupting her work. Good Lord. If they only knew that her heart was beating triple time against her ribs.

"Well, since you stole my song, the least you could do would be come up here and sing with me," he slurred. For heaven's sakes, the man was half drunk. And geez, could his jeans get any tighter? *Focus, Kylie.*

"Excuse me, sir. You mean to tell me you sing a song about bein' a single girl that can't be tied down?" The audience cracked up all around her.

"She's cute, Clive. Where'd you find this one?" Trace bellowed across the bar. Kylie didn't look to see what Clive did, but she could see a few cell phone screens lighting up the room. This was definitely going to be on YouTube. Trace Corbin was going to make sure she never got recognized in the industry, unless it was by people laughing at her.

"Well, pick a song already. I got tables to wait on," Kylie said, hopping back onto the stage.

He eyed her carefully as he lifted his guitar. "You gonna change the words all up? Make me look like a fool?"

"Oh no, darlin.' Pretty sure you can handle that all on your own," Kylie answered with a flirty grin.

She prayed she looked like she was keeping her cool, but the last time she'd seen this man he was on CMT and she was watching from her bedroom in Okla-fricking-homa. And holy hell if he wasn't even hotter in person. He smelled like aftershave and bourbon. Kylie decided then and there that she'd never be able to get a whiff of either without recalling this moment.

Trace played a few cords and winked at her. She just shook her head. Whose friggin' life was this? She recognized the song immediately. *Waitin' for You to Call*, one of his "booty call ballads," Lulu called them.

"It's two am, can't believe I'm back here again. We called it off again tonight, just like all the other times. But we both know it wasn't right."

The deep timbre of Trace's voice sent unwelcome shivers through Kylie's body, but she launched into her half of the lyrics. *"I've got the T.V. turned down and my ringer up loud, waitin' for the sound that says you've come around. Can't wait to hear your voice as you say those words, the ones that always cause me to fall. I'm here waitin,' waitin' for you to call."*

Kylie knew she didn't do as well as she had done when she sang on her own. Her voice shook a few times and she could barely concentrate on the lyrics with the famous singer watching her so closely. So she just stared into the bright lights and pretended she was singing to her daddy in Heaven as they harmonized on the chorus.

"I know you didn't mean the things you said, know you didn't mean to leave my bed. You said you couldn't do this anymore, said you didn't want to try. But I know you, and this is just another lie."

She took a second to pull air into her lungs while Trace sang his part. *"The sun's comin' up and my heart is breaking down. I'm still waiting for that sound that says you've come around."*

Softening her voice to imitate the way she'd heard him sing the next verse on the radio so many times, she sang her final solo. *"You don't have to say you're sorry. I forgive you. I won't have to say I love you, 'cause you already know. We won't waste time apologizin', just pick up the phone."*

With her heart thrumming louder than the music, Kylie let her voice flow into his as they sang the final chorus together. *"I'm here waitin', waitin'. I'll be right here waitin', waitin'. I'm still waitin' for you to call..."*

She should've just thanked the audience, hopped down off the stage, and resumed her regularly scheduled life. But she didn't. Instead she made the colossal mistake of looking over into hazel eyes that had darkened to the color of the sky just before a deadly twister touched down, destroying everything in its path. She was from Oklahoma and she knew a thing or two about storm warnings. Trace Corbin was setting off all the sirens inside of her. Kylie was standing directly in the path of something wild and dangerous and a hell of a lot more powerful than her. *Look away*, her subconscious screamed. But she couldn't, because for the first time since her daddy died, she was alive.

KYLIE did everything she could to try and behave like a normal human being for the rest of her shift. She waited tables, filled drink orders, and ran drinks for waitresses on break. She rolled her eyes when Tonya gestured maniacally at Trace Corbin and a few other men who were sitting in a back booth with Clive.

"That was seriously amazing. I mean, *wow*," Tonya told her with wide eyes as they cleaned the hospitality room. "Trace's band still hasn't cleared out of the green room. And by the way, he was totally giving you fuck me eyes on stage."

"No he wasn't," Kylie said, feeling her cheeks heat because she couldn't help but wonder what *was* going on in that glare of his.

"Yeah he was," Tonya said with a laugh. "And I mean it, you held your own." The woman didn't even attempt to keep the awe out of her voice. "That chick I told you about going on tour, she couldn't hold a candle to you."

"Whatever, I think you need to go home and get some rest. I got this." Kylie shooed her away saying, "Think of your cute little kiddo in her little pink jammies."

Tonya paused near the door. "I'm just…I'm afraid I'll never see you again," she said quietly.

"Unless Clive fires me, you'll see me tomorrow."

But Tonya just shook her head and then crossed the room to give Kylie a hard squeeze.

I am so fired, she thought as her friend hugged her tighter.

"Don't get pregnant," Tonya whispered in her ear, and then she was gone.

Okay, weird.

THE employee lounge was empty when Kylie settled in to wait for Trace Corbin and his band to vacate the green room so she could start cleaning up. Her heart was still beating a bit faster than usual from the night's odd twist of events.

She couldn't stop replaying the scenes over and over in her head. If this was how working at The Rum Room would be, hectic, unexpected, and amazing, she could see herself being happy here for a long time. A wide smile was still stretched across her face when Clive came in, looking similar to how Ms. Pam had the day she let Kylie go. *Of course.* In her life, everything that seemed to be too good to be true always was.

"Well, little lady. I have to say, you surprised me this evening," Clive told her, wiping his sweaty brow and sinking into the couch next to her.

"Good surprise or bad surprise?" she asked, using all the self-control she had not to bite her lip.

Clive chuckled in response but didn't answer. "There are some men out there that have a proposition for—"

"Oh no, Tonya already told me about those men," Kylie broke in.

"Not *those men*, Kylie. Trace Corbin's guys."

"Um, am I like in trouble or something?" She gave in and chewed her bottom lip. *Geez, could the guy not handle a little sarcasm?*

Her boss laughed again and shook his head. "For heaven's sakes girl, they want to talk to you about touring with him."

"What?" Kylie figured this had to be a joke. And not a particularly funny one.

"Look, Trace is a good kid. I've known him a long time but lately things have been—"

"I know," she interrupted quietly. "I watch TMZ."

"Right, so here's the thing. It's your life and this is a huge break. I'm not too old to see that. But you're young and talented and I can make some calls. It's not like this is your only shot, understand?"

Her mind couldn't even fully accept that this was really happening in order to answer. Trace Corbin's "guys" were about to offer her some kind of a deal. But Clive was advising against it, sort of. *Too much to process,* she thought to herself while trying to regulate her breathing. Her hopes were on the verge of soaring out of her reach but Clive's warning kept them hanging on, even if it was by a thread.

"So you think I should tell them 'thanks, but no thanks'?"

Her boss heaved out a sigh. "I can't tell you what to do. You seem like a smart girl, and if you decide to go…then I'll understand. You will always be welcome here to play music or to wait tables or whatever you want."

"Thanks, Clive. Seriously." She paused for a second and then added, "He doesn't like me very much, does he?" She said a silent prayer that she wouldn't have to clarify.

The older man cleared his throat so loud it sounded painful. "It's not about that. And if it does start to be about that, then you need to get the hell off that tour."

chapter SEVEN

LIKE the ghost of dreams past, the girl staring back at Kylie was a stranger. So many times she'd dreamed of performing in front of a packed house. And now here she was, about to live her dream.

Straightened silky blond locks flowed over her shoulders framing perfect skin and clear blue eyes that were wider and brighter than they'd ever been. The spray tan, facial, teeth whitening, and full body wax she'd had to undergo had peeled away plain old Kylie, and underneath was *Kylie Ryans*, fresh-faced newcomer touring with Trace Corbin.

It was her first show as Trace's opening act. Pauly wanted them to do a song together, but Trace wasn't interested. In fact, Trace was pretty much non-existent.

The morning after Trace's big night at The Rum Room, Lulu had called shrieking with excitement about seeing Kylie and Trace on the Internet. Kylie had told her friend about the offer from Trace's guys.

Despite the arguments she'd built up in her head and the long list of reasons not to run off and jump on a fledgling tour, Lulu had cut clean to the point. "No offense, Ky, but what have you got to lose?"

A cold hotel room and a waitressing job, albeit a pretty good one. Seemed stupid to turn down a legitimate offer from a once platinum album-selling superstar. Plus, there were only six shows left on the tour. How bad could it be?

So far, pretty damn bad.

The first time she'd stepped onto the huge bus, the smell of leather and expensive men's cologne nearly overwhelmed her. Running her hand lightly over a marble countertop, she stopped abruptly when she saw Trace Corbin sitting in the circular booth across from the compact kitchenette area she had to walk through to get to the room she'd been told was hers. Like a gauntlet.

"Mr. Corbin," she said softly, mentally slapping herself for how much of an intimidated kid she sounded like.

He didn't stand up, didn't shake her hand, or even offer her a head nod in greeting. No "Welcome to the tour," or "Mi casa su casa." Nothing. Just steely eyes raking over her, appraising her and finding her lacking. He raised an eyebrow and leaned back in the booth, taking up as much space as possible. As if to say he was king of all he surveyed and she was taking up too much of his time and too much room on his bus.

Well, she wasn't looking for a new BFF. She could deal. She quirked a brow of her own, passing him quickly. And then she hid in her tiny room for the rest of the evening.

Giving up on the fitful version of sleep she'd been working at, she sat up in the middle of the night somewhere between Nashville and Dallas. The bus was stopped and she could hear men arguing. Kylie tried lying back down and closing her eyes to block them out until she heard something that sent her heart pounding. Her name.

"Seriously, this is the best you could come up with? A waitress from nowhere fucking Oklahoma? If I'd have known this was going to happen, I never would've pulled the little twit up on stage," Trace's cold voice said. Kylie tried to ignore the jagged blade of hurt carving into her. Well, she'd been called worse. The insults Darla had slung at her when she'd kicked her out had included words she didn't even know the meaning of. *Whore* was one of the ones she knew. Kind of ironic since Kylie was still technically a virgin, not that her stepmother would believe that. She jumped at the sound of something crashing against an interior wall of the bus and thudding to the floor.

"Look, I get that this isn't the ideal situation. But what the hell did you expect? There was the debacle with The Pretty Pistols, you punched Bryce Parker in the face, and then you broke the little American Idol girl's heart and tossed her out like yesterday's garbage. You're not exactly playing well with others, here, and frankly...you're out of options."

Kylie didn't hear his response but she had just learned a great deal about Trace Corbin. Turns out he was kind of an asshole. *Figures.*

Great, she thought, relaxing her crouching position and resting her head on the wall next to her. *I'm on the tour from hell and everyone else has been smart enough to get off.*

The morning after her eavesdropping, Kylie was getting some fruit from the kitchen when Trace stumbled in. Pauly was doing something on his iPad in the curved booth. "Was that the last banana?" Trace asked as she began to peel her breakfast.

She stopped mid-peel. "Maybe. You want it?"

"Yeah, I do," he said, practically growling at her.

"Well, you can have it," she relented, tossing him the banana, even though she couldn't remember the last time she'd eaten. "On the condition that in the future, you keep your late night, whiny baby, celebrity crap to a dull roar so the little twit can get her beauty sleep." Kylie paused to glare at the man across from her. "Think you can manage that?" Pauly's head snapped up and they both waited for Trace's reaction.

Trace glared back but the corners of his mouth twitched. "I can try," he said evenly.

"Yeah, well, don't hurt yourself, superstar," she said as she sauntered past him into her room. Screw it. She wasn't that hungry anymore anyways.

If he responded to her it was drowned out by the sound of Pauly's hysterical laughter.

Since then he had been polite. Distant, but polite, which Kylie was more than fine with. But now there was an hour before she was supposed to go on stage in Dallas, and Trace Corbin was nowhere to be seen. While staring at her almost unrecognizable reflection, she had a feeling he was going to make damn sure her dreams never came true.

Like hell.

chapter EIGHT

"GET off the stage!"

"We want Trace!"

"Go back to Oklahoma, waitress! Hey, get me a beer first!"

Kylie had been on stage for over an hour. Her set was only forty-five minutes and the crowd knew it. Pauly's voice had come through her ear piece demanding that she stall both times she'd tried to wrap it up. But the patrons at The Blue Moon knew a hack job when they saw one. She was out of material and the crowd was about to get violent.

"I'm so sorry, Trace can't be here tonight. He's—"

An amber glass bottle whizzed past her head before she even had time to think up a decent excuse for his absence.

"Pauly!" she shouted as two security guards converged on a man in the back. Pauly appeared and escorted Kylie off stage. She was shaking. Not from fear. From anger. Trace Corbin was going to get an ear full. Whenever he turned up.

IT was nearly three in the morning when Kylie heard the bus rumble to life. They were scheduled to perform in Baton Rouge tomorrow night.

If the bus was moving, he was on it.

Kylie burst out of her room and started to storm to the front of the bus but stopped halfway. Trace was strewn across the booth in the compact kitchen.

"Fun night, Mr. Corbin?" she asked him. The beautiful mess in front of her lifted his head, hair flopping over one eye. He threw her a wicked grin before answering, "Yeah, yeah it was."

"Good, I'm glad. Because I got booed off stage and had a beer bottle thrown at my head. So at least one of us had a good time."

If she thought she was angry before, she was nearing homicidal. The cocky jerk laughed. Freaking laughed, as if the thought of beer bottles being hurled at her while she was booed was the perfect end to his night. No 'I'm sorry,' or even 'That sucks,' just outright laughter.

"I'm glad I amuse you, but in the future if you can't be bothered to show up to your own damned show, feel free to give a girl some notice." Kylie started to stalk back to her closet of a room, but she was still boiling. And she was determined not to lose anymore sleep over this selfish jackass. No, she was going to rage on, getting it all out until she was exhausted.

"No, you know what? Here's what really burns me. There are people out there, real people, with kids they can barely feed, and bills to pay, and rent, and real problems. And they show up to work day after day, night after night. But you, with your money and your flashy bus and your tight ass jeans, you show up whenever you feel like it. Or not. Like there aren't a million people out there who would step over their own mothers to be in your shoes. And you know what else?" She sucked in more air so she could finish.

Something resembling pain flashed across the man's face at her last comment but she couldn't stop. Words tumbled out so fast she barely had time to think. "You probably have about fifteen more minutes until some guy with deeper dimples and tighter jeans, if that's possible, comes along and steals your thunder. Because really, you're not all that damned special. But congratulations. I hope it makes you feel like a big man to leave me and Pauly high and dry while you go out and have a good time."

"You done?" Trace's eyes were only half open. The red tingeing Kylie's vision was fading slightly.

"No, I'm not, but I think two more seconds would be too much time to waste on some pathetic drunk who pisses away God given talent for his own amusement."

At that, he sat up, squaring his shoulders and leveling her with a cold stare. "Oh yeah, and what the hell do you know about it?"

Oh, wow. He was just spraying her fire with gasoline. Kylie lowered her voice and leaned close enough to smell the liquor emanating from him. "I know that I thank the good Lord that I'm not a fan of yours, because the only people you treat worse than me and Pauly are your fans—or maybe your band members who'd rather travel crammed into the Winnebago behind us than be this close to you."

"Really waitress, that the best you got? If I'm so pathetic, why don't you just run on home to Daddy now?" He cocked his head and folded his arms across his chest.

Tears stung the backs of Kylie's eyes, but no way was she going to let this guy cut her any deeper. Snapping back as if he'd slapped her, she tried to keep her tone light. "You know, I would, but he's been dead for seven months. And it's a good thing for you because if he was alive to see you destroying everything I've worked for, you'd be in a world of pain."

"Shit, I didn't know—" Trace interrupted himself to scrub a hand over his face.

"Makes no difference," she snapped. "But I can tell you this much. Your ass better show in Baton Rouge because one of us actually wants to be here. And I'll be damned if someone like you is going to piss all over my dream before I've even had a chance to live it." She knew she was snarling. Good. Maybe he would realize that she wasn't screwing around. "I could care less if you like me, or respect me, or give a damn about me, Mr. Corbin. But this is my shot and everything I've ever wanted and—"

And that was all she had. She shook her head, trying to convince herself not to cry. One more word and Kylie would break down in humiliating sobs. So she turned on her heels and escaped to her room.

chapter NINE

TRACE was the one who'd stayed out drinking all night, but Kylie woke up with the headache. *Naturally.* She sat up and tried to get her bearings. Why was she awake so early?

Screaming. She could hear the screaming of someone on speakerphone filling the bus. Leaning against the wall by the bed, she heard a man's voice she didn't recognize. And he was pissed.

"…how much that fucking costs? Paying back the venue, the vendors, refunded tickets? That shit is coming straight out of your pocket, Corbin!"

The low rumble of Trace's response was unintelligible. But the man on speaker was loud and clear. "One more screw up of any kind, I mean it. One more dramatic meltdown, or underage girl saying you screwed her, or if you are so much as two seconds late to a sound check, you are done, Corbin. And I don't mean just with this tour. I mean with the whole goddamned label!"

Trace shouted a few obscenities, and something that sounded like *motherfucking puppet,* causing Kylie to wince. Pauly murmured something in a soothing tone and then she heard Trace storming off the bus.

Jesus.

Lying back down, she practically broke a sweat trying to fall asleep again. Trace was going to ruin everything. And he was taking her down with him.

She must've dozed off because when she sat up and checked her phone, it was nearly ten. From the sounds outside of her door, it sounded like Pauly was talking to Trace and things had calmed down. She tried hard not to feel nervous about facing him after her huge blow up, and then having eavesdropped on someone from the label tearing him to shreds earlier this morning, but there were angry butterflies battling it out in her stomach all the same.

A text from Tonya said Clive had come through on his promise; she was scheduled for some studio time as soon as the tour was over. Kylie was supposed to have three original songs prepared. So far she had one.

Rehearsal on stage in Baton Rouge wasn't until two so she figured she'd try to get some writing done until then. She took an Excedrin and stumbled to the restroom on the bus. Surely she would feel better after a hot shower.

AFTER showering and working up enough nerve, Kylie headed into the sitting area on the bus with her notebook and plans to get some lyrics down. She nearly tripped when she saw Trace eating breakfast in the booth where she'd confronted him last night.

"Um, morning," she mumbled.

He responded by holding up a box of cereal like a shield.

"Like that would save you," Kylie deadpanned.

"Apology accepted. You wanna talk?" he asked with a mouthful of Fruit Loops.

She was starting to think Trace Corbin had drunk himself stupid. "To who?" she asked as she grabbed a banana. Someone had restocked. She switched on the Keurig and leaned against the counter.

"To me."

She narrowed her eyes at her nemesis' clear hazel ones. "Pass," she said, turning back to the coffee maker. It wasn't like there was anything else left to say.

"Come on, I'm not really that bad. Promise."

"Oh yeah," Kylie began as she added sugar to her coffee cup. "Says who?"

"Yeah, okay," Trace answered with a shrug before he shoveled in another mouthful of cereal. "I am sorry about Dallas. Saw it online." She might have imagined it, but it seemed like he flinched. "That was brutal." Except his mouth was full of cereal so it came out "bootal." God, he even talked with his mouth full. If only all the women who threw their underwear on stage at his concerts could see him now.

Kylie slid into the booth across from him and glanced at the colorful bird on the box. "What are you, eight years old?"

"Emotionally, yes."

She sipped her coffee, glaring at him over her mug. "Then it all makes sense."

Trace stopped chewing and gaped at her. "You always this mean?"

"Well, that depends. Are you always this selfish and unreliable?"

"Not always," he answered with a dark look. He pulled his fitted navy blue baseball cap off, ran a hand through his thick hair, and slipped it back on backwards. He hadn't shaved. Something about the scruff on his chin made Kylie's stomach tense.

"We'll see."

She took another drink and flipped open her notebook. She didn't really want to write this close to this man, but it was the only comfortable spot on the bus.

After a few minutes, Kylie was lost in lyrics. She'd been thinking a lot about Tonya and women like her. Hardworking single moms who did everything they could to provide for their kids but had to sacrifice time with them to make ends meet. She jotted a few phrases from conversations they'd had and tried to wrap them into a chorus. After she had that part worked out, everything else just started to flow. She needed her guitar. She hopped up to get it, startling when she saw Trace staring at her from behind the sports section of a newspaper.

"Can I help you, Mr. Corbin?" she asked politely, making a conscious effort not to grit her teeth together.

"You gotta stop calling me that. It's Trace. Or my friends call me Tray."

"Trace it is then," she clipped as she headed back to retrieve her guitar. As soon as she stepped back into the little kitchen, her heart stuttered and her blood froze in her veins. He was leaning over her notebook.

"Jesus, what's with you?" she asked, snatching her songbook back from him.

He didn't appear to be apologetic for invading her privacy. "Kylie, you've got some decent stuff there, seriously," he told her.

"Surprised?" she asked, responding to his tone more than his words.

"Well, yeah. I mean, what are you? Eighteen, nineteen?"

She didn't see what her age had to do with anything. "Your point?"

"My point is, for a few more weeks, you're on tour with someone who knows this business. If you ever wanted to run stuff by me, I'd be open to it."

"Noted," she told him, returning to her lyrics.

"I'll leave you to it then," he said as he slid out of the booth.

THEY were performing at some place called The Texas Player's Club, which given the recent nightmare that was Dallas, Kylie was feeling pretty nervous about. She supposed it was a good thing that Trace was on his *Back to My Roots* tour when she joined since the venues were relatively small.

After hair and makeup had transformed her into *Kylie Ryans*, she got off the bus, heading towards the bar to rehearse. When the two-story wood-slatted building came into view, she nearly tripped over her own two feet. "Pauly, what the hell?" she demanded at the band manager she hoped would be hers one day. She tried her best to keep her voice down but she was a panicking mess on the inside.

"What's wrong?" he asked, stroking his graying goatee and stepping away from the band members heading into the bar in front of them.

"Um, this place is freaking huge. Thought this was a small venue tour, intimate settings and all that?" She thought that because that's what she'd been promised.

"Yeah, this one's a little larger. But it's nothing to worry about. It's a fun crowd, mostly college kids. You'll be fine."

Right, more people to throw beer bottles at my head. Kylie sincerely hoped none of the local college's baseball players would be in attendance.

After she finished with sound check, Kylie found Pauly on his phone outside by the bus. She'd seen Trace watching her on stage, so she knew he'd at least shown up for rehearsal and sound check this time. Not that he couldn't still disappear in the next two hours.

She waited quietly while Pauly finished up his conversation.

"Okay, yeah, I know. We've discussed it. He wasn't interested until today but I think it's gonna happen." He smiled at Kylie and gave her a hang-on-a-sec gesture with his hand. She nodded.

"On whose album though?" There was a long pause and then he nodded, as if the person on the other end could see him. "Yeah, okay. That's what I thought too."

Kylie examined her manicure.

"There will have to be some major thawing out, but progress is progress. I'll update you as we go. I'll be in touch." Pauly ended his call and turned his attention to her. "What can I do for you, Kylie?"

"I just wanted to tell you that tonight, when my set is over, I'm getting off the stage. If your boy is a no-show, you can go out there and apologize for him and they can throw stuff at *your* head."

"Yes, ma'am. Understood," the manager said with a nod.

She turned to walk away but Pauly called out after her. "Wait! Hey, Kylie. Your wardrobe options are hanging in your closet."

She nearly laughed out loud when got back to her room and unzipped the sleek black garment bags. There were three choices—a short red sequined dress that was a size too small; an even shorter black skirt with a white lace top, if you could call the scrap of fabric that; and a pair of designer jeans with a dark blue t-shirt with a faded American flag that said *Pride* across it.

Door number three, she thought to herself. She knew there was a lady who picked out their performance stuff, but Pauly had to have gotten the t-shirt. He was the only one who knew the name of her hometown. It was cut so low that she wished she had time to dig through her suitcase and find a tank top to put on under it. But when she put it on, a smile spread across her face. She could do this. Lulu would be proud of her. Maybe her dad would be, too. Though he might not have approved of the top.

"TRACE?" Pauly called from the front of the bus.

Kylie was already dressed so she stepped out of her room.

"Kylie, you seen Trace?"

"No, not recently, why?" No he was not doing this again. *No fucking way.* Pauly muttered something equally as harsh under his breath and stomped off the bus. Her mind raced. What was his freaking deal? Was he trying to get dropped from Capital Letter Records, the biggest damn label in Nashville? Whatever, not her problem. Him pulling another no-show where the audience would blame her and then the tour getting canceled before she could blink, that *was* her problem.

Kylie racked her brain as she made her way to the bar. Surely Pauly had checked the green room. Some bars, nice ones like this, had private party rooms for VIPs only, according to Tonya. If she could get into the one here at The Texas Player's Club, she'd drag Trace Corbin out by his ass, stick her arm up it, and do his entire set ventriloquist style if she had do.

Pushing through the crowd, she found a back hallway backstage similar to the one at The Rum Room. After several failed attempts, she found a locked door with voices, mostly high-pitched female ones, coming from within.

Freaking hell, she did not want to think about what was happening on the other side of that door. But she had to get in somehow. Yanking a bobby pin from her hair, she took a deep breath to brace herself for whatever lewd acts she might be about to witness. Just as she was about to pick the lock like her dad had taught her to do in case she ever forgot her house key when he worked late, a male voice from behind her stopped her.

"No need to pick the lock, sweetheart. Pretty girl like you can come in as my personal guest."

Kylie turned slowly, trying to keep the guilt off her face. The man was tall-ish, though not as tall as Trace, and he looked to be about her age. Something about his bright blue eyes, black hair, and wicked tattoos swirling up his thick muscular arms was vaguely familiar. "Steven Blythe," he said, winking at her. "Hero for a Night," he added.

"Um, I don't need a hero. I just need—"

Dark laughter made her insides quiver. "Hero for a Night is the name of my band. We play here a lot, though tonight we're just here to see Trace."

"Oh, right. I knew that." Kylie's cheeks heated as the man she now recognized from the cover of last month's *Rolling Stone* magazine let his eyes dip to the swells of her breasts protruding from her low cut top.

"Here," he said, producing a key from his pocket and opening the door. "Welcome to the Player's Club."

If she thought she was embarrassed about her little faux pas with Steven Blythe, she was downright mortified at what she was walking in on. It was like the seventh circle of hell, if the devil was a porn director.

Half-naked girls pranced around, some serving drinks on trays, some wearing nothing more than trays, like x-rated cigarette girls. While others were busy giving full on lap dances. Several men sat around drinking and smoking cigars, some of them too involved in conversations to even notice the girls.

"Stay close to me," the guy from behind her murmured.

Happily. Things had taken a strange turn as the guy who'd startled the shit out of her five minutes ago now seemed like the safest bet. "I need to find Trace. He's due on stage for sound check, like now, and..." *And we're both out on our asses if he's late*, she wanted to add. But she didn't want to go around telling Trace's business to strangers.

"That him over there?" her new friend asked, pointing to a man across the room wearing a trucker hat, watching two girls go at it on a couch with a bored look on his face.

Trace sat alone, swirling dark liquid in a glass and looking for all the world like he owned this sin haven. Kylie needed a shower after just walking through it. "Yeah, thanks." She meant for that to be Steven's cue to go about his business. She didn't even want to think about what that business might be in a place like this. But he followed her over to Trace.

"You were due on stage ten minutes ago," Kylie informed him as she approached, doing her best to keep her eyes off the two women groping all over each other next to him.

Trace's jaw went slack as he took in Kylie walking towards him. His eyes hardened noticeably when he saw Steven close behind her. "Kylie? What the hell are you doing in here?"

"She came in with me," the guy behind her said. She could hear the arrogant smirk in his voice.

"Well get her out of here," Trace sneered, a threat hardening his words.

"No," she broke in. "I'm not going anywhere until you do. You heard what they said. If you're late to sound check, you're done. We're done."

Trace didn't respond, just stared at her and then glanced around. When he stood, Steven backed off, but she didn't. Kylie watched his chest heave in and out, and something in her ached to touch him. Maybe she was a little turned on by all the blatant nudity and sexual tension in the room. Maybe Trace's smoking hot self being so close she could feel his breath on her, had her brain rewiring itself to accommodate the lust filling her head. Maybe she was losing her ever-loving mind.

"Turn around and walk out of this room. *Now.*"

Looking up into his eyes, she waited until he pressed his gaze into hers before she spoke. "Not without you. I'm not leaving this room until you do." Her voice was breathy and weak but her nerves were steel. She glanced around at a few of the men noticing their heated exchange. She winked at one of them. "Maybe we should stay, Trace," she drawled. "Bet I can find a few handsome fellas willing to buy a girl a drink."

"You're underage," he offered evenly. The sweet sting of bourbon filled her nostrils.

"They don't have to know that, and I can tell a few of them don't mind. Might even prefer it."

Before she had time to decide how far she was willing to take this, Trace's hand gripped her upper arm roughly and she was being pulled from the room. A few whistles pierced the air and she knew how it looked.

Like she was a jealous girlfriend yanking her man from the clutches of temptation. Though, technically, he was the one practically dragging her from the room. But she didn't care. He'd be on stage soon and the label would keep the tour going. For now at least.

IT was nearly midnight when Trace wrapped up and finished signing autographs. Kylie noticed a redhead and two blondes hanging around as if they were waiting for him. She couldn't help but wonder if Trace would bring them on the bus. Surely he had more respect for her than that. Not that she really cared who he shacked up with, but she didn't want a front row seat either.

Maybe it was better when he didn't show. Big Red was inching closer to Trace by the second. Hello, desperate much? *Ugh.* Kylie was too keyed up to go sit on the bus anyways.

"So what's it like going from waitressing to this?" a deep voice asked from behind her.

Kylie whirled around to see who the speaker was. Steven, her hero for the night. She grinned up at him, though still slightly embarrassed about the scene he'd witnessed earlier.

"Haven't really had a free second to think about it," Kylie told him, leaning back so she could get a good look at him. Lulu would've swooned all over herself.

"Kylie Ryans, not just a waitress, even though that's how she introduced herself as she was backing away from me," he read from a copy of *Country Weekly*.

"What? Where does it say that?" She made a grab for the magazine but the tattooed Adonis before her lifted it just out of her reach and kept reading.

"But though she seems modest and shy at first glance, don't be fooled. On stage she transforms into a vixen, full of swagger with a deep southern sound that will captivate any audience."

"Does it seriously say that?"

"Wait, there's more," he told her, holding up a hand. *"Kylie has confessed to having a thing for tatted up musicians, specifically those in country rock crossover bands."*

"Let me guess. Hero for a Night specializes in country rock crossover?" She couldn't help but grin.

"Thankfully, yes. Quite a coincidence, huh?"

Kylie rolled her eyes and turned to leave. She really wanted to get back to the bus so she could get online and find out how she ended up in *Country Weekly*.

"Hey wait, you want this?" he asked, stretching the magazine out to her.

"Um, I don't want to take it from you since you carry it around and all," Kylie told him with a smile.

Steven laughed and handed it to her. "Nah, I'm not much of a reader. Just grew up with Trace and heard some girl he was touring with might be mentioned in this issue. Wanted to see if this Michael Miller dude knew what he was talking about."

"And did he?"

"Yeah, I think he did." He looked around and shoved his hands into the pockets of his jeans. "Actually I was going to see if you wanted to come to a party with me now that you're all done here, and Trace is behaving himself."

"Um, I don't think—"

"Don't think you'd be safe with a tatted up guitar player? You might be right," he told her with a wink.

"Hardly. It's just, I'm not really sure if my, um, Pauly, would be okay with that." On one hand, a party sounded kind of fun and it would probably be a lot better than the ones back home. And it would definitely be better than witnessing the Trace and Big Red flirtfest. But on the other hand, she didn't know this guy or the area. Probably not a great idea to go off on her own.

"Okay, well, *your Pauly* could come too. That your boyfriend?" Something dark flashed across his handsome face, but he smiled.

"No, he's my, I mean Trace's, manager." Saying Trace's name out loud forced him to the forefront of her mind. She glanced over her shoulder to see him laughing and tossing back shots with the redhead. The blondes were nowhere to be seen.

"Well, if he's hanging with Shelby, he'll be at the same party we're going to. Surely if he can go you can too, right?"

Kylie watched as Trace helped *Shelby* off her stool and they headed out of the bar. Excellent point. "Can't see why not," she answered with a shrug.

"Sweet. I need a Ladderball partner." Steven draped an arm over Kylie's shoulders and steered her towards the exit.

"I have to be back to the bus before tomorrow morning. We leave at six."

"I'm scandalized," he said dropping his arm, mouth gaping open at her. "Here I am asking you to a party for a few drinks and some innocent Ladderball, and you're suggesting a sleepover? I barely know you."

"Shut up. You know what I meant!" Kylie shoved him lightly, but she was kind of glad he'd dropped his heavy arm off of her shoulders.

"Uh huh. I know how you famous types are. I'll probably wake up tomorrow feeling used and alone."

"And wondering where your wallet is," she added with a mischievous grin. "Wait, I have a question. What the hell is Ladderball?"

LADDERBALL, as it turned out, was much harder than it looked. Especially after a few shots of something purple that made the Earth tilt. And it didn't even involve a ladder, which made it all the more confusing.

Kylie and Steven played against the lead singer of Hero for a Night, Ben, and his girlfriend, a raven-haired chick named Gina. It looked like PVC pipe and balls on a string, but there was some complicated scoring system and Kylie couldn't keep track of who was winning.

"Are we winning?" she asked her new friend, who was swigging his Michelob from the bottle and smiling at her with a playful gleam in his eyes.

"No, darlin'. We're pretty much getting killed," he told her with a shrug. Gina high-fived Ben and did something that looked like a drunken victory dance.

"Can we go play something else?" She had seen some couples playing beer pong and a bunch of girls playing flip cup, and she'd rather play either.

"We can go find an empty room and play doctor if you'd like," he said quietly.

Kylie's head swam. She didn't really know where she was, only that they had walked to the party from the bar. Dread and regret pressed down on her. "Actually I need to find a restroom," she informed him.

"Come on, I'll show you." He reached a hand out to her, so she took it. Kylie played it cool as Steven led her up the stairs to a tight hallway, though the whole night was starting to seem like a pretty shitty idea. Just before she started to panic and flee back downstairs, he gestured to a door on the right where two girls were propped on the other side, looking moments away from puking.

She did have to pee, but she also wanted to text Pauly the address and ask him to come get her. Steven seemed harmless enough, but it was nearing two in the morning and the crowd was thinning out. Kylie had heard enough stories from girls at her high school about what happened at college parties. At the very least it was going to get awkward. And she was tired and pretty heavily buzzed.

Just as she pulled out her phone, a Hispanic guy with a buzz cut burst out of the bathroom, sending the other two girls in line reeling backward. "You do not want to go in there ladies. Sorry," he said before staggering toward the stairs.

"Oh gross," one of the girls groaned as she peeked into the restroom.

"I know where there's another one," Steven told her, taking Kylie by the elbow.

The other restroom was down another dark hallway and through a messy bedroom. Kylie darted in quickly so Steven couldn't follow. As soon as she'd closed the door, she pulled out her phone and started to text Pauly. Except, oh for heaven's sakes, she'd forgotten to get the address from Steven first.

"Hey, Steven?" she called out.

"Need some TP?" he answered back.

"Uh, no. I was just wondering, whose house is this exactly?"

"It's the Phi Kap house, why?"

Okay, that was less than helpful. But Pauly was smart. Surely he could figure it out. "So, are you like a brother here?"

His deep melodic laughter sounded from the other side of the door. "Nah, some buddies of mine from high school are brothers here. I'm not really the college type, sweetheart."

Kylie prickled a little at this random dude calling her sweetheart. After a minute passed, he called out, "Everything okay in there?"

"Peachy, thanks." She peed quickly and washed her hands, leaving the water on as she texted Pauly. **I'm at the Phi Kap house (?) and am not sure how to get back to the bus. Don't really know anyone well enough to ask for a ride or walk back. Come get me?** At least that's what she'd tried to text, but the new phone Pauly had given her was touch screen and her hands were still damp...and she was maybe more drunk than buzzed.

The message she actually sent looked more like **Im a Phkao ?? not sure how bus don't kno anyone enough ride back come gee mee?**

"Kylie?"

"Be out in sec."

The thought of stepping out into that dark bedroom with an extremely sexy and very intimidating stranger twice her size, that she barely knew, was making Kylie nauseous. Or maybe it was the shots. Or the beer. She splashed some water on her face and tried to recall the saying Lulu was always reciting at parties about beer and liquor. Which order meant you were in the clear and which one made you sicker?

She stared into the mirror waiting for her reflection to be still.

"Hey, there's someone in there. What the hell are you—"

Kylie heard a man swearing outside the bathroom door as she tried to focus on the screen of her phone. God, why wouldn't Pauly just text her ba—

The bathroom door burst open and she jumped to avoid getting hit. Trace stood there, eyes blazing and chest pumping. Steven was behind him, holding his shoulder and looking pissed.

"Let's go," Trace growled at her.

What the hell was he doing here? She decided to ask him. "What the hell are you doing here?"

He stared at her as if he was gaging her blood alcohol content with his eyes. "Doesn't matter. Let's go."

"Um, okay. I texted Pauly and—"

"Kylie, we're leaving now. Either you can walk or I can carry you out."

Before she could really process what he was saying, Steven stepped inside the now way overcrowded bathroom. "She's fine, man. I can get her back to the bus before—"

He didn't get to finish his sentence before Trace's knuckles connected with his mouth.

And then Kylie was airborne and upside down over Trace's shoulder. As they bounced down the stairs, she felt the vomit rising in her throat. Oh God. She was about to puke on last year's Country Music Artist of the Year. In front of an entire fraternity. Definitely not her finest moment.

"Put me down," she ordered as soon as they were outside.

He didn't. Instead he asked her a question through clenched teeth. "What the hell were you thinking?"

She groaned and closed her eyes so she wouldn't have to watch the sidewalk blurring by. Though it meant giving up an excellent view of Trace Corbin's ass. "Right now I'm thinking I'm going to be sick."

Thankfully, he set her down gently on the sidewalk. Kylie leaned towards the bushes lining the concrete and violently relieved her stomach of the chicken salad sandwich she'd eaten before performing. And all of the purple stuff she'd drank, judging from the looks of it.

"Oh my God," she moaned when she was finished. This was why she was always Lulu's DD.

She stood up and felt her hair fall around her. Trace must've been holding it. The sweet acidic smell of vomit wafting from the bushes was too much. She took a few wobbly steps backward, strong arms steadying her from behind. "Well, at least I didn't puke on you," she said, looking up into his face. The hat he wore cast a shadow making it impossible to see his eyes. For some reason this bothered her. He had the prettiest eyes.

"Yeah, thanks. This is my favorite shirt."

Kylie glanced at the faded plaid button up he wore. "Why?"

"Wow, even drunk you're snide and hateful. I'm impressed."

She flushed and fumbled for an apology. "I didn't mean it like that."

"It's okay. That's one of the things I like about you actually," he told her with a shrug.

Her skin prickled but she wasn't sure why. It was pretty warm out and there wasn't even a breeze or a chill in the air. The extreme awkwardness of the situation settled between them as they walked away from the fraternity house. "So...did you score with Red?"

Trace turned to face her but kept walking. "Who?"

"The redhead you left the bar with. *Shelby*?" Kylie hoped it sounded like she was just making casual conversation. She was irritated and had no clue as to why.

Trace laughed so loud it made her head hurt a little. “No. Why? You jealous?”

Her face went hot and she knew it was probably glowing with humiliation. Thank goodness it was dark out and the streetlamps dotting their path weren't bright enough for him to see her. Because *oh hell*. She *was* jealous. And very stupid, apparently.

“Yeah, I am. I'm really into redheads.” She prayed he would just drop it. No such luck. He stopped dead in his tracks behind her. “Joke,” Kylie assured him, turning to grin at his slightly open mouth.

“Hey, it's okay by me if you're into girls,” he told her as he began walking again. “It would explain why you seem to be repelled by me. Actually, it would do wonders for my ego.”

chapter TWELVE

As they climbed onto the bus, Trace offered her a hand. Even hazy from the alcohol, she was aware that his touch singed every nerve ending in the palm of her hand to life. She overheard Pauly arguing with someone on the phone. Or at least, she assumed he was on the phone and not shouting at someone in person. Thankfully his room was up front so she wouldn't have to deal with him too. She desperately needed to brush her teeth and wash her face. A shower sounded great but like it might be too much work. Being drunk was exhausting.

Trace helped her back to her room. She turned to thank him but he disappeared out the door before she could say anything. Stripping off her clothes, she decided to take a shower after all. She grabbed a towel and wrapped it around her. Just as she reached to open her door, it slid away from her.

"Thought you might—" Trace began but stopped when he took in Kylie's state of undress.

"Um, thanks," she told him, reaching out to take the bottle of water he held in his outstretched hand.

Her towel slipped down a few inches as she sipped the water. She couldn't help but notice that Trace looked away. She remembered his words from earlier. He was wrong. She wasn't repelled by him. In fact, judging from the way he was refusing to look at her, even to so much as sneak a peek, it seemed more like it must be the other way around.

AFTER a hot shower, she felt a lot better. Still slightly woozy, but better. Mentally berating herself for getting into such a stupid situation, she pulled on a tank top and a pair of girly boxers. Steven had seemed nice, but something about the look on his face when she'd mentioned Pauly and the playing doctor comment had made her uncomfortable. Thank goodness Trace had shown up when he did.

Just as she was about to lie down, she realized she hadn't ever actually thanked him. Punching the poor guy was probably over the line, and her less than graceful exit had kind of pissed her off and made her sick, but Kylie knew good intentions when she saw them. She owed him a thank you. She hated owing people. So she threw the covers off and got out of bed.

She crept out into the hall and past the kitchen. Trace's door was shut but she could see light from underneath. *Just go back to bed and thank him tomorrow.* But she really didn't want to mention this night ever again. So she knocked softly.

"Come in," she heard a muffled voice say.

A small lamp on the bedside table and the bluish glow of a flat screen television lit the room. It took her eyes a few seconds to adjust. But when they did, oh. *Oh.* Trace sat shirtless in a chair by the enormous bed. He had taken one boot off and was working on the second.

"Hey," she began as the entire purpose for this late night visit slipped right out of her mind. His second boot hit the floor with a soft thud.

"Hey," Trace answered, standing and shoving his hands in his pockets. "What can I do for you?"

"Um, wow, your room is huge," she blurted out.

Trace chuckled softly. "Yeah, for a bus I guess it is."

Fill the awkward silence, idiot, a voice in her head commanded. "Um, so how'd you get to the party so fast?" she asked.

Trace's eyes tightened. "Uh, Red, as you called her, gave me a tour of the campus. I'd just dropped her off at her dorm when Pauly forwarded your text. I was actually just about to pass by there."

"Oh, well um, I'm glad." Oh crap, that made it sound like she was glad he wasn't with Red. Which she was. But no need for him to know that. "I mean, I'm glad you happened to be nearby. Not that I wasn't okay or anything, but I didn't exactly know how to get back to the bus."

"Okay," he said evenly, his eyes meeting hers with an intensity that had her backing up.

Okay, Kylie, just say what you came to say and freaking leave already. "Why did he send my text to you?"

Trace smiled. "Probably because I speak fluent drunk in person and on text, and he knew I was on campus."

Jesus. Her text had alerted Pauly that she was drinking. Great. "Oh. Was it that bad?"

He didn't answer her question, just slid his phone off the night table and touched the screen a few times. Before Kylie had time to figure out what he was doing, he handed it to her.

The jumble of letters looked nothing like what Kylie had meant to send. "I told Pauly I didn't need a new phone." Even though she kind of did since her refurbished hand-me-down from Lulu barely held a charge. The man had insisted, saying they would take it out of her tour pay. She suspected he was lying.

Trace smirked at her. "Uh huh, 'cause the phone made you drink or what?"

"You know, I'm starting to think you should've been a comedian."

"Maybe in my next life," Trace said with a sad smile that she couldn't understand. "Is that what you came to tell me?"

"Not exactly."

Trace cleared his throat and Kylie wondered how many girls he'd had in that huge bed. At least one that she knew of—the American Idol chick. Kylie had Googled her. Mia Montgomery. She was pretty. Okay, gorgeous. The official release said she had left the tour for personal reasons. Well, Pauly seemed to know exactly what had happened, so it wasn't that personal after all.

"It's late, sorry. I should get back to my room." Kylie reached back for the door handle.

"Kylie?" Trace's deep voice sent a spasm vibrating up her spine. She froze with her fingers on the handle.

"Yeah?"

"You're welcome, and don't sweat it. We've all been there."

It took her a few seconds to figure out if Trace was being genuinely sweet or irritatingly condescending. His eyes were warm but his mouth twitched. *Hmm.*

She was just about to say goodnight when he took a step and lessened the distance between them. She thought he'd stop when he got within arm's reach, but he kept coming. He didn't stop until she was backed against his door and they were practically touching.

His handsome face merely inches from hers, a faint hint of his trademark bourbon scent teased her. Despite her previous resolution to never touch alcohol again, she was overwhelmed by the desire to taste the liquor on his lips. "Kylie, if I ever again see you in a place like The Player's Club, or alone in a bedroom with a musician who wants nothing more than to fuck you, then I can't be held responsible for what I might do."

She swallowed hard, resisting the urge to shrink away from the intensity of his stare. "Does right now count as being alone in a bedroom with a musician who wants to fuck me?"

Her words surprised them both. Trace leaned back just slightly. She watched as his eyes widened and then narrowed. "Yes, it does. Which is why you should run back to your room as fast as those pretty little legs can carry you. And lock the goddamned door."

Adrenaline surged hot and powerful through her entire body. Heat flooded between her thighs, weakening her knees. Biting back a surprised whimper, she refused to break eye contact first. Trace gave in, letting his eyes lower to take in the way her tank top hugged her breasts.

Oh, God, she wanted him so bad it hurt. Wanted him—no, *needed* him—to touch her like she could tell he wanted to. But he motioned for her to move aside, so she did. She watched helplessly as he opened the door and nodded her dismissal.

Fine, she wasn't going to beg. "Goodnight, Trace," she said softly.

A dark warning flashed in his eyes as she realized it was the first time she'd called him by his first name out loud. He held the door open for her. Her body screamed at her to wait him out, to ask him to give her what she needed. But her pride wouldn't allow that. So she slunk back to her room and collapsed onto her bed. She didn't lock the door, and that throbbing ache was pulsing for her attention. Why did he have to be so damn hot? The man exuded raw barely controlled power and overwhelming heat. His skin would probably sear hers on impact, but damn she wanted to touch him.

Since watching Darla parade men in and out of her bedroom, treating her like the trash that she was, Kylie had sworn off the opposite sex. She focused on working her ass off to keep the bills paid, and working on her music took up all of her time anyways. She didn't know what it would feel like for a man to please her, but she damn sure knew how to please herself. She was a virgin, not a nun.

Slipping under the covers she closed her eyes and pictured him. Him sitting in the Player's Club VIP room, his eyes only sparking to life amidst all that sex when he saw her. Him bursting into that bathroom to rescue her in his own way. Him pinning her to the door with his stare and telling her he wanted her.

Her hands weren't masculine and strong like his would be, but that's what her imagination was for. Sliding her fingers down to herself, she groaned and whimpered as she grazed her sensitive flesh. Her body rocked hard off the bed as she dipped into her wetness and slicked it around her folds.

Sex with Trace would be rough, she knew from the way he grabbed her in The Player's Club, but she'd bet he could be gentle too. He sat her down outside the Phi Kap house like she was made of glass. His scent lingered on her, that sharp, clean cologne and something else woodsy and warm that was just *him*.

She overheated as her orgasm ramped up. She was losing control, wishing she had thrown herself at him moments ago when she had the chance. God, he would feel so good inside her. She was going to come fast, something she'd never been able to manage, often leading her to just give up or avoid this altogether. But this time it felt wonderful to let go. Tortured moans escaped her throat without her permission. She was so damn wound up all the time. For once she just wanted to let go.

So she did. And oh, dear Lord. Amidst her raging cries, she called out his name. Once, twice, and a third time on a sigh as she came back down to Earth with a shudder. The white hot blanket of shame at the realization of what she'd just done covered her.

Burying her face in her pillow she begged the universe to be kind to her for once. *Please, please tell me he didn't hear that.* Something thrown hard against a wall—a chair maybe?—jolted her entire body almost as hard as her orgasm had. He'd heard all right. And he was pissed.

chapter THIRTEEN

SHE was making coffee in the small kitchenette when he emerged from his room the next morning. Her entire body flushed so deep it was painful. Before she could think of something to say that might ease the tension between them, Trace stepped in close behind her. Bracing his muscular arms on either side of her, effectively trapping her between him and the counter, he leaned in and let his breath tickle her neck.

"Sleep well?" The rumble of his voice sent a tremor through Kylie's shoulders.

"So well it should be a sin," she drawled, using her heaviest accent while turning in his arms to face him.

A low growl escaped his throat and the heat in his eyes neared lethal. "Did you lock the door like I told you to?"

Kylie bit her lip and shook her head. She'd disobeyed a direct order. She sincerely hoped there would be a punishment in her near future. Preferably something involving spanking.

"You're really testing me here. I don't recommend it, darlin'." The bourbon lingering on his breath pulled her from her lust-filled haze. The scent was more potent than it had been the night before. Alarms rang out at the realization that he was already drinking this early in the morning.

Once he turned and headed towards Pauly's room, Kylie nearly crumpled to the floor. The breath she'd been holding rushed out of her as she tried to regain some sense of composure. Shaking her head, like that would actually clear it, she wondered what she had been thinking. She wanted a career, a chance to make a name for herself. Not to be another random girl Trace Corbin bagged in the sack and tossed out on her ass.

As much as she didn't want to concern herself about him, she was still feeling pretty grateful that he'd cared enough to punch a guy out on her behalf. Even if it was totally unnecessary. The way his eyes had flashed and his fists had clenched, it was like he was *worried* about her. Why, she had no idea. But it felt nice since the only other person who'd ever really cared that much was buried in Oklahoma. As she searched the cabinets for tea and honey, she opened one that she hadn't even noticed before.

Bottles of liquor, the good stuff that probably cost more than she'd make on this tour, or maybe ever, filled the bottom shelf. Jesus. The man could open a package store. A half empty pint of Johnnie Walker Blue Label caught her eye and she lifted it. There was a tag still attached to the neck.

Trace, Great show! Can't wait to have you back in the Blue Grass State! Your friends at the Brass Bull. Another, a single malt scotch Kylie had never heard of, sat behind Johnnie with a tag attached as well. *Looking forward to working with you again! E & C Recording.* Half a dozen bottles of Heaven Hill bourbon sat behind the fancier bottles, a few with cards and tags on them like the others. Did these people not think about what they were doing? For the love of all that was holy, the man was *known* for getting drunk, getting in trouble, and damn near tanking his recording deal. *Nothing says 'thank you' to an alcoholic like a big ass bottle of expensive liquor.* Nice.

Anger surged violent and hot, and an impulse Kylie couldn't control struck her. She grabbed the bottles and began pouring them down the sink one by one. *So he doesn't screw up this tour and ruin it for me*, she tried to tell herself. But the real motivation behind her actions? Something she didn't want to think about. Or admit. Tears began to stream down her face as quickly as the liquor was going down the drain. *Did no one care enough about him to realize what was going on?* At the very least, they should've cared about his music and tried to stop him from spiraling out of control.

When she was finished, she stared at the empty bottles on the counter. All twenty-seven of them. Her hand rose to her mouth as she took in the aftermath of her temporary insanity. What had she done? More importantly, *why* had she done it?

"RELAX, Pauly. It's one damn drink."

Kylie was sitting in the booth on the bus attempting to write when she heard him coming. She'd thrown the evidence of her psychotic break in a black garbage bag and tossed it in a dumpster behind the bar in Jackson they were performing at in less than an hour.

The voices got louder as they stomped onto the bus. "Trace, you heard what Noel said. If you're so much as—"

"Back the fuck off, Pauly. I'm having a drink on the bus so no one runs their mouth to Noel. Then I will go in there and blow the damn audience away like I always do. Your paycheck is safe." The snide tone wasn't one she was used to hearing him use with his manager.

Forcing herself not to look up when he came towards her and yanked the cabinet doors open, she fought hard to overcome the nauseating waves of dread rolling over her.

"What the hell?" Trace didn't acknowledge her, but he whirled on Pauly like a man possessed. "I swear to God, if you emptied my liquor cabinet, your ass is fired."

Kylie's head snapped up and she watched as Pauly held up his hands in a gesture of innocence. Trace was closing the distance between them. She recognized the beginning of a physical confrontation when she saw one. Apparently so did Trace's manager, who began backing up as quickly as Trace was approaching.

She couldn't let Trace fire his manager. Pauly was most likely the only reason he still had a career at all. Sliding out of the booth, she steeled herself for the full force of the fiery rage about to be heading her way. "Pauly didn't empty your cabinet. I did." Her voice sounded a whole lot stronger than she felt.

Confusion contorted Trace's features as he turned to face her. "That's real cute, Ryans. Where'd you hide it?"

Biting her lip, she realized he and Pauly were blocking the only exit. Her heart sped and a cold clammy sheen of sweat covered her. "I didn't hide it. I poured it down the sink."

Trace's eyes went wide. And then anger darkened his entire presence. She didn't know what Pauly was doing because she couldn't see past the man advancing on her. "Tell me you're joking. Tell me now." Trace's low growl was enough to break her resolve.

"I would say I'm sorry," she whispered. "But I'm not."

Rage radiated off him. Nostrils flaring and chest heaving in and out, he backed her against the booth. "Is this because I didn't fuck you?"

Kylie's face began tingling and she lost all feeling in her legs. *This must be what it feels like to go into shock.* "No. It's not. And you're an asshole for bringing that up and you know it." Kylie lifted her chin and bit the hell out of her bottom lip so it wouldn't quiver. "I did it because you have a drinking problem. And because no one else would."

"Listen to me." Trace punctuated each word with a heavy breath. "You and me, we're nothing." He waved a finger between the two of them. "Whatever you've built this up to be in your pretty blond head, that's all it is. In your head."

The truth hurt, even though she'd known it all along, but she swallowed the pain and squared her shoulders. "Okay. Now you listen to me," she began, taking a step forward and forcing him to back up out of her personal space. "I thought I'd made myself clear. I don't want a single thing from you. Hell, I don't even *like* you. But for right now, and for the next few weeks, I need you to be sober and not ruin the rest of this tour like you seem to be dead set on doing. If I so much as get a whiff of liquor on your breath on the day of a show, I will go straight crazy-ex-girlfriend-psycho-bitch on your ass. And I will dump any and all liquor I find on this bus."

"The hell you will," he threatened, pressing back into her space. Kylie glanced around him for some assistance, but Pauly was nowhere to be seen. Great.

"And what are you going to do about it? Have me kicked off the tour? I'm sure the label would side with me since they're not interested in paying for any more of your no-shows. When this tour ends, you can drink yourself right out of your career for all I care."

"Who the fuck do you think—"

"Trace, that's enough. She has to be on stage in five minutes." A soothing male voice broke through the tension and cut him off. Pauly and a guy named Danny from Trace's band stood at the front of the bus. Kylie breathed a sigh of relief. She leaned to the right and darted around him but his hand struck out and gripped her arm, pulling her back in his direction.

"Trace," she whimpered, both angry and a little afraid as their eyes met. "You're hurting me."

Shocked remorse flashed in his eyes and she almost wanted to comfort the bastard. But he released her so roughly she stumbled in her attempt to get as far away from him as she possibly could. Pauly met her halfway down the aisle and rushed her off the bus while Danny stayed behind to deal with the fallout of her actions. Her traitorous body trembled as they walked to the bar, but she was glad for what had happened. It had served to destroy any hopes she had of getting to know Trace Corbin in any capacity.

DESPITE the drama in Mississippi, the show actually went well. Afterward, Kylie had to sit down with Cora Loughlin, Trace's publicist, who was in town specifically to me with her. Now there was a woman she didn't envy.

Cora's suffocating floral perfume filled the tiny space of the media room on the bus as she helped Kylie set up artist Facebook and Twitter accounts. They also posted some videos on YouTube and linked them to Trace's *Back to My Roots* tour website.

"Not to be dense, but what exactly am I supposed to say on these things?" Kylie asked. She already felt like a slug next to Cora with her sleek suit and perfect hair. Kylie had her writing jeans on with an old t-shirt that was a size too small and featured Hank Williams Jr's face. It was her favorite. She put on a scarf, arranging it just so to try and hide the stains. Not that the elegant woman seemed to notice or care.

"Oh, you know. Just how excited you are to be touring with Trace, how great the crowd is at each show. Stuff like that."

"Um, okay. Why?" Kylie couldn't figure for the life of her who in the world would want to "follow" what she had to say online. She'd had a personal Facebook back home but she only had like a dozen friends on there from high school and she never really updated it with anything other than pictures of her and Lulu goofing around.

"Post some photos of you and Trace being silly on the bus, whatever you're eating, teasers about songs you're working on…Just light fun stuff, okay?" Cora waited for Kylie to nod in agreement and then went back to looking at something on her iPhone. She didn't want to tell the woman that all she and Trace had been doing together on the bus was avoiding one another since their screaming match.

"Not sure she does light and fun, but I'm sure she could fake it. Right, Kylie?" Trace leaned in the doorway of the media room polishing something against his shirt. Fake it? Did he think she'd just been faking him out the other night? Maybe that was better than him knowing the truth about her little fantasy. Or was he making fun of her because he was still pissed about the alcohol? Whatever. Trying to figure him out was not on her list of things to do at the moment.

"Look," Cora began, glancing at Trace and then back to Kylie. "This is the way people connect with you and it's how we build some chick from Oklahoma that no one's ever heard of a fan base. If you don't feel like you can do it, let me know and I can get one of our tech guys to keep up your account. Okay?"

"I can do it," Kylie mumbled, feeling like Trace had just called her an uptight reject, and Cora, who'd known her for all of an hour, concurred.

"Great." The publicist beamed and smiled, blasting her pearly whites out from behind her bright red lipstick. "You have my info. Call me if you need anything."

"Trace," Cora nodded to him on the way out.

"Cora," he said curtly as she passed.

Kylie wasn't stupid. She saw the tension that passed between them. Apparently Cora was more than Trace's PR lady. Geez, did this guy hook up with everybody? Well, not everybody. He hadn't so much as joked about anything remotely like hooking up with her since the night she had to tear him from the VIP room at The Texas Player's Club. But after seeing American Idol girl and Cora, it wasn't like she could compete with his type anyways. Oh, wonderful…the last thing Kylie needed to be thinking about was competing with his women. *Gross.*

Kylie felt like she'd been staring at Trace forever, but thankfully only a few seconds had passed. She knew she needed to say something, try to make things better—or at least less awkward. But no words came so she busied herself with balancing the laptop on her legs. There definitely needed to be a table in the media room.

After she'd scrolled through her online profile, she Googled herself. All that came up was her new Facebook account, a YouTube video of her and Trace at The Rum Room that she'd already watched with Cora, and something Capital Letter Records had released about her being added to Trace's tour. She clicked to the videos she and Cora had posted and was shocked to see that they already had several comments. She scrolled through them and tried not to freak out since Trace was still leaning in the doorway, eating an apple.

Guess this is who Corbin is banging now.

Girl can sing, hot little body too!

She's totally lip-synching! What a wannabe!

Heard she was a waitress. Hello blondie, time to go back to your day job!

I like her! She's pretty and what an awesome voice! Heard she totally showed Corbin up at a sing off at a bar where she worked or something.

How can you even understand what's she singing? Sounds like she's just repeating the chorus over and over. Nice tits though.

And then there was one Kylie couldn't even process. And not just because of the misspellings. It was posted by someone called CunTreeSux and it was awful. Kylie shuddered and started to slam the computer shut. Trace's hand shot out and gripped the screen, startling her. She hadn't even heard him come closer.

She glanced at him quickly, noticing that his eyes were hard as he scanned the comments. His warm breath grazed her neck and the side of her face as he leaned in, setting her body on high alert.

"Don't Google yourself, ever. I mean it," he said.

"I just wanted—"

"I'm not saying that the social media stuff isn't great for your fans—it is. But there are some whack jobs out there and some just plain assholes that get off on slamming someone else. I mean, you see any of them baring their soul in front of several hundred people every night?"

"No," Kylie said quietly, sitting the computer aside and turning to face the man beside her. "Why do I even have to put this stuff out there if people are just going to write such horrible things about me?"

Trace shrugged and took another bite of his apple, taking the time to chew and swallow before speaking again. "It's supposed to be for people who like your music, but nine times out of ten the people who comment just want to tear you down. I don't know why, but who gives a shit? It's their problem, not yours."

She knew what he was saying made sense but the comment where someone had said they'd heard her sing and would rather hear baby pigs being tortured still had her cringing inside. And that one comment. *Freaking hell.* It made what Darla had said to her seem like a compliment.

"Look, I know I'm the last person you want advice from, but you have to have a really thick skin for this. Like superhuman thick, because that's what this is. You put yourself out there the night you got on stage at The

Rum Room. And you will be out there from now on unless you decide to walk away from it." Trace took another bite of his apple and stood. As he turned to leave, Kylie fought the urge to reach out to him for comfort. She wanted him to wrap his arms around her and tell her that everyone was crazy and those people were wrong about her.

And if she was being honest? She was relieved that they were back on speaking terms. Even worse, she wanted him to look at her the way he'd looked at Cora. And probably Mia Montgomery. And maybe more than once.

"Trace?" she called out just before he disappeared from sight. He didn't say anything but he turned around and met her gaze from the doorway. "You're not the *last* person." *And I forgive you.* Kylie smiled to let him know she was grateful for the advice. Trace grinned and nodded just before he disappeared.

chapter FOURTEEN

THE Wild Hog Saloon in Mobile, Alabama, was a barbecue bar and grill joint that reminded Kylie of home. Not only did she and Trace both play to a packed house, but the owners brought them dinner personally and told them to make themselves comfortable long after the show was over.

Pauly had friends in town that he was staying with for the evening. Kylie couldn't help but feel nervous about sleeping on the bus with Trace all alone all night. Somehow with Pauly there it had seemed like there was a chaperone. Or at least one responsible adult to keep things from getting out of hand.

She joked around with the male bartender as she ate her mouthwatering pulled pork barbecue sandwich and drank sweet tea that tasted like nectar from the gods. She tried not to notice that Trace was a few seats down with a bottle blonde she didn't have a clear view of. Determined not to give a shit, she focused her attention on the guys in Trace's band instead. They hadn't paid much attention to her when she first joined the tour. Kylie figured they didn't expect her to be around long, so she didn't take it personally. But lately they'd all been a lot warmer.

Davis Lowe, Trace's guitar player, busted out a very professional looking poker set at one of the round tables near the bar. Mike Brennen, the bass player who Kylie suspected was a recovering alcoholic since he always got club soda with a lime wedge, groaned at the sight of it. "Dude, you gonna make me kick your ass again? You were such a bitch about it last time."

All of them glanced in Kylie's direction as soon as Mike let the b-word slip.

"My bad, Ryans," Mike muttered. His messy blond hair was almost covering his eyes, but Kylie could tell there was a genuine apology in there somewhere.

She rolled hers and shrugged.

The guys carried on with their trash talk while Kylie finished her food. When she was done, she slipped off her stool and pulled up a chair in between Ken Lackey, the drummer, and Danny Brees, the older man who played the fiddle and had witnessed the incident in Jackson. Not because she preferred them to any of the others, but because she could still see Trace from there. She didn't even realize what she'd done until after she sat, and she kind of wanted to bitch slap herself for it.

"Uh oh, little girl at the big boy table," the heavily tattooed drummer teased.

"Maybe one of you big strong boys could teach me how to play," Kylie drawled. She was flirting a little, but she'd watched them play a few times before. She was pretty sure she could kick each and every one of their asses at Hold 'Em. She bit her lip to keep from smiling.

"If you sit on my lap, I'll let you look at my cards," Mike offered. *So he's the flirty one then.* Kylie liked to assess her opponents' personalities so she could tell when they were bluffing, when they were getting twitchy, and when they were getting cocky.

"Stay right here, sweetheart. You stay away from that one. He's bad news." Danny was gray-haired but handsome in a Patrick Duffy sort of way. Kylie smiled at the older man. She was going to feel kind of bad about taking his money. Maybe she'd work out a signal with him so he didn't get swindled like the rest of them were about to.

"Twenty-five to play, *sweetheart,*" Mike informed her with a wink. She smirked at the come on. As he dealt Kylie in, she allowed herself a peek over at Trace. He and the blonde were coming closer, moving a few stools down to watch the game. Homegirl's boobs were definitely of the silicone variety.

"Trace, aren't you going to show me the bus? I've never seen the inside of a big music star's tour bus before." The woman's high-pitched nasally voice grated on Kylie's nerves.

She snorted out loud. "I bet she's seen the inside of a *whole lot* of buses," Kylie blurted without thinking. All four of the guys at the table gaped at her. "Oh shut up. You were all thinking it," she said quietly, hoping Trace wouldn't hear.

Mike made the mewling sound of an angry cat, but Kylie ignored him. Her face burned with the shame of her public jealousy.

Much as it nearly killed her, she lost the first four hands. Lost them badly. Danny gave her a sympathetic smile and offered a few pointers about checking instead of upping the ante. "Sometimes it's better to fold. Doesn't mean anything. Just means you were dealt some sorry cards."

Story of my life, Kylie thought to herself. "Right, yeah. I need to remember that," was all she said. She did her best to look confused and nervous as the other men upped the pot. Mike was winking at Trace's blonde, who was sneaking him seductive little smiles in return, so Kylie figured he didn't have a very impressive hand. Davis was turning a chip between his fingers, fidgeting. Waiting on the river card because he needed something specific, she would bet on it.

Ken was the wild card. He didn't flirt, fidget, clear his throat, shift his weight, or make eye contact. Just stared impassively at the cards on the table like he was bored with the whole thing each time he added his chips to the pot.

The river card was the Queen of Hearts that Kylie needed to clench her royal flush. This was it; she was taking these suckers down. *Little girl her ass.*

She let the boys up the pot a little more before letting out an exaggerated yawn. "Wow, I'm beat. Can I just go all in and call it a night?" Kylie asked.

"Aw, leaving us so soon?" Mike asked with a wink.

"Kylie, if you go all in and lose, you'll owe these guys a hundred bucks," Danny cautioned her. "And they take this stuff seriously. They've had to take out loans to pay each other back."

Mike laughed. "We'll give you a free pass this time, babe." It was the *babe* part that had Kylie planning her victory dance in her head.

"No, that's not fair. I've gotta learn somehow, right?"

"Trace," his company whined his name as she pouted. "After she loses she's going to the bus, then we won't be all alone." Clearly she'd meant for Kylie to hear. Guess she wasn't the only one with her claws out. Glancing up, she could see why the woman was getting pissy. Trace hadn't taken his eyes off Kylie once in the last few minutes.

She squirmed under his stare but returned her attention to the game. "Aren't y'all tired? That was one hell of a show you guys put on tonight. Maybe we should all go all in and hit the hay." She jerked her head towards Trace without looking at him. "Looks like I might be bunking with y'all tonight," Kylie said. "Think there's room for me?"

"Hell yeah," Mike said, shoving his chips into the pot with enough force to knock a few others off the table.

"Trace?" The startled tone of the bar fly's voice had everyone looking over.

Trace was leaning forward and glaring down at the whole group of them. "That winnebago's packed full, Kylie. You'll sleep on the bus."

Kylie ignored him and slid all her chips to the middle. "We'll see. I might have to work out a payment plan with these boys if I lose."

Trace mumbled something incoherent under his breath as Ken and Davis went all in. Danny was chuckling beside her.

"Sometimes it's better to fold," she whispered under her breath. Danny grinned and nodded as he placed his cards face down.

"Show me yours and I'll show you mine," she drawled.

Mike winked at her as he laid down the two cards that, paired with the cards on the table, gave him trip fives. Ken had nothing. But Davis had a full house.

"Sorry darlin'," he said as he showed his hand.

"Aw man, I don't even have two that match," Kylie complained, turning her Jack and King of hearts over. She slid them right next to the other three cards on the table that completed her hand.

"What the fu—,"

Danny's laughter interrupted Mike's curse and made Kylie smile, forcing her to give up her façade. "Oh, well I'll be. That's a royal flush, isn't it?"

She made a big show of taking everyone's money, thanking each of them as they handed it over. Then she wiggled her hips in her version of a victory dance. "Ah, guess I'll go take a long hot shower and count my money in bed. Nightie night, fellas."

"That's some bullshit right there," Ken announced.

Mike was a little more adamant, though his tone was edged with disbelief. "That girl just swindled the piss out of us."

Danny was still laughing as Kylie gave him the hundred bucks he still had in chips. Her daddy had taught her to play when she was just a little girl. He'd also taught her not to screw over decent people. "Yeah she did." Danny winked at her as he took his money.

Davis was apparently okay with being hustled by a girl. "It was almost worth it to see that sexy little victory dance."

Kylie turned to leave, planning to walk right past Trace and his date for the evening.

"What, no goodnight for me?" His eyes were dark, that same stormy color they'd been in Nashville.

She stopped and turned to face him. "Good night, Trace," she said softly, purposely ignoring the daggers the blonde was glaring at her. "If you're going to have, um, company, I might go sleep in Pauly's room so you can have some privacy." The words were acid in her throat. But the thought of hearing Trace and the woman hanging all over him made her sick. She almost shuddered hard enough for him to notice. Maybe she'd sleep in that Winnebago after all.

Trace opened his mouth to say something, but Kylie cut him off with a hug neither of them was expecting. "You can do better," she whispered in his ear before turning and walking away as quickly as she could manage without making her desperate need to escape obvious.

HER end of the bus was still quiet when Kylie got out of the shower. She didn't want to think about what might be going on in Trace's room.

Buttoning up a faded blue oversized work shirt of her dad's that she liked to sleep in, she fought off the pangs of longing and nostalgia that playing poker with the guys had brought on. Her dad had taught her how to play because he had his buddies from work over the first Saturday night of every month for poker night. He wasn't always able to find a sitter to keep her entertained. Plus, nothing beat the look on a grown man's face when a ten-year-old girl conned him out of half his paycheck. Those guys learned pretty quickly not to let her play after she'd gotten them all at least once.

She left her hair wet, letting the mass of curls dampen the back of her shirt as she propped up in bed and tried to write. Every time a lyric popped in her head, Trace's turbulent stare replaced it before she could write anything down. Then her dad's gentle laughter, like Danny's tonight, filled her head and her chest with that familiar soul-deep ache.

For a girl who'd just won nearly four hundred dollars, she felt like crap.

She'd already brushed her teeth, but she had a hankering for hot tea. She'd seen a box of powdered chai tea latte mix in the cabinet on the bus. It would have to do.

Running lights on the floor illuminated the interior of the bus just enough to keep her from falling and breaking her neck on her way to the kitchenette. She reached out and felt around for the switch under the cabinets that lit up the area above the sink. She had just flicked it on when Trace's bedroom door opened.

Her heart stuttered and Kylie froze. If the woman from the bar was in there with him, Kylie was taking her ass to that Winnebago dressed just as she was.

Taking a few deep breaths to brace herself, she turned. Trace stood in the doorway, his dark shirtless figure making her heart race.

"Couldn't sleep," she said softly. He just stared at her, reminding her with his scorching gaze that she was dressed in a thin nightshirt that barely reached her thighs. "No company tonight?" she asked, doing her best to keep her voice light, unaffected.

Trace said nothing as he stalked towards her slowly, the force of his stare backing her against the counter.

"Trace," she said softly as he came close enough to touch.

Still nothing. Just his eyes burning into hers as his bare chest expanded with each breath. His hair was a mess, like he'd spent all night raking his hands through it, and he was barefoot in jeans. Kylie was pretty sure this was the hottest she'd ever seen him. Heat flooded her body, liquefying the lust between her thighs.

The sensation became so intense it was almost painful. Before she had time to ask him what he was doing, Trace's strong hands gripped her and lifted her onto the counter. His labored breathing was the only sound she heard as he used those same hands to spread her knees apart. Kylie whimpered when he moved forward to press himself between them.

This was not the Trace Corbin she was used to. This man had pleading eyes and was trembling to the point of vibrating with…want. Or maybe it was need. Kylie wasn't sure. The muscles holding her rigid relaxed under his warm hands. He trailed them up her thighs, to her hips, finally reaching up and touching her face with gentleness she hadn't expected him to be capable of. His thumb grazed her bottom lip and it sent a shock straight through her, causing her to arch into him.

"You played those boys tonight." His quiet ragged voice raked over her.

She couldn't speak, so she nodded. *Yes.*

"You been playing me?" He pinned her with an intense stare she struggled to return.

This time she shook her head no.

When he let his hands fall back to her hips, she reached up and placed her fingers in his hair, using the lush brown locks to pull him closer. His head dropped below hers with a soft moan, and she could feel him breathing her in. She took advantage of the opportunity to do the same. Bourbon, aftershave, and that woodsy scent that was all Trace. No cheap perfume from his friend from earlier. Trace's soft warm lips brushed against her neck, sending another shiver through her with so much force it would've jolted her off the counter had he not been holding her in place. "I'm sorry about what happened in Jackson," he whispered. "God, I'm so sorry." His voice was thick and raw and broke something inside of her.

She still couldn't manage to get any words to reach her mouth, so she just gripped him tighter. She'd already forgiven him.

Her mind raced with questions. The most pressing one being, *what the hell are we doing?* But somehow it didn't seem important to figure it out right that second. She wanted this, ached for it. She hadn't even realized how badly until that very moment. Holding him close to her felt right. Safe. As if this was what she had needed all along. This is what would take the pain away.

Trace pulled away, just a few inches, but Kylie moaned her displeasure. She tried to pull him back in, biting her lip when he shook his head. God, those eyes. *Take cover*, they said, because the storm was here, now. And Kylie wanted nothing more than to hurl herself right into its path.

She didn't know what he was looking for, but his eyes sought answers in hers that she didn't have. She didn't even know what the question was. She just wanted him. Like she had never wanted anything or anyone in her entire life.

Cupping her chin firmly, Trace leaned in and oh, *oh* she was more than ready for his mouth. But he didn't kiss her. He pressed his forehead to hers and closed his eyes. "So damn beautiful," he rasped.

Gripping his hips and pulling him as close as possible, until the only thing keeping them apart was the thin lace of her panties and the denim of his jeans, Kylie let her hand stroke his stubbled cheek. She pulled her legs up to wrap them around his waist and Trace let loose a deep growl that had her throbbing against him. The intimacy of it was like nothing she'd ever experienced, taking her higher than even performing on stage had. Trace Corbin should come with a warning label: *highly addictive*.

Just as she turned her face to him, ready to demand his mouth, he stiffened and jerked completely upright. As if he'd been in a trance, he shook his head and looked at her like he didn't know how he'd ended up in this precarious situation. "You can do better, too," he said quietly before he turned his head away from her. His deep voice was pained, laced with an emotion Kylie wished was lust but suspected was something else.

"Trace—" she began, but he tore himself out of her tangled grasp and walked back to his room, closing the door behind him and disappearing as quickly as he'd materialized in the doorway.

A wave of conflicting emotions slammed into her so hard she nearly fell to the floor when she tried to lower herself to standing. Kylie held the edge of the counter to keep herself upright. Forget the tea. She had to get back to the safety of her room so she could spend the rest of the night trying to figure out what in the hell had just happened.

chapter FIFTEEN

WHEN they arrived at the The Dixie Tavern in Georgia, Kylie was relieved to see it was about the same size as The Rum Room. But Trace was from Macon, so the bar was filling quickly. She'd just finished her sound check when she spotted a pair of girls heading towards the bus.

Annoyance and jealousy gripped and pulled her in opposite directions. Trace hadn't so much as looked at her since their odd encounter last night. To make matters worse, the two attractive dark-haired women just strolled onto the bus in front of Kylie like they owned the place.

Laughter was already trilling through the tight space when she stepped on. Quietly, she made her way to her tiny compartment and changed into her performance outfit. Feeling self-conscious about some of the things she'd read about herself online before Trace had stopped her, she chose a loose fitting silver one-shouldered dress with black leggings and boots. She put on the jewelry that went with it and headed out. She could warm up in the bar's green room and not have to deal with Trace's groupies. Thank you very much.

"Kylie?" She heard his voice from behind her just as she passed his room. Great.

"Yeah, um, I'm just heading in to warm up a little, give y'all some privacy." When she stepped into Trace's doorway she saw that the older woman was standing near his bed and the younger of the two sat on his lap. Something twisted inside of her. Maybe last night had never happened. Maybe she'd dreamed it. But every time she looked at him she was right back there. Clinging onto him for dear life. It had seemed like he was doing the same. That part she definitely must have imagined.

"Is this her?" the brunette with a pixie cut on his lap asked. No way she was older than sixteen.

"Yeah, it's her," Trace said with a smile, clearly feeling no shame about his little fan club.

The petite girl jumped off his lap. "You're even prettier in person. Can I have your autograph?"

"Um." Kylie looked to Trace. Who was this chick?

"Sorry, she's kind of a pest," he said with a slight lift of his shoulder.

"Hey!" The girl gave Trace a firm shove.

Kylie just stood there, trying to figure out what in the world was going on.

"Guess I should introduce you," Trace began. "Kylie, this is my little sister Rae," he said gesturing to the shover. "And this is my older sister, Claire Ann."

"Oh, hey. Nice to meet y'all." She tried to ignore the relief that flooded through her as she shook each woman's hand.

"Seriously," Rae began, "I have watched the video of you annihilating my brother at The Rum Room like fifty times." The girl's smile lit up her entire face.

A grimace flashed across Trace's, but his eyes were full of love for his little sister. She'd yet to see him look at any other woman that way. Well, maybe her for just a second last night. But it was dark and she might have imagined that, too.

"I don't know if *annihilate* is the right word." Kylie couldn't help but smirk a little.

"No, it is," Trace confirmed.

"We're just happy that Trace finally found someone who can put up with him," Claire Ann said with a warm smile in his direction.

"It's not easy," she said, winking even though she was completely serious.

But then she thought about him rescuing her from the Phi Kap house and how he didn't make her thank him. He hadn't even gloated a little.

And he could definitely have humiliated the hell out of her if he wanted to. He'd definitely heard her that night.

"Looks like you may have met your match, little brother," his older sister said as she leaned down to kiss him on the cheek. "We'll get out of here, let you two have some space before the show."

"You're coming tonight, right? Both of you?" Rae asked on her way out. Kylie had no clue what she was talking about.

"We'll see, Rae," Trace answered. His forehead wrinkled, and Kylie could tell that whatever she'd invited them to wasn't something he was particularly excited about.

"Nice meeting you, Kylie, and I'm serious about that autograph," Rae called on her way out.

"You too, um, both of you, and okay," Kylie said with a smile.

Trace sat on his bed looking slightly embarrassed and a little...proud, maybe? One thing was for sure—he looked much younger after the short visit with his family.

"So, those are my girls," he said with a shrug. "Rae's a little wild but you just have to love her."

She smiled. "Yeah, I got that." Okay, time to vacate his bedroom now. She felt like she'd just invited herself into an intimate family gathering, even though she knew she hadn't really. But there was something she wanted to know. She hadn't checked online and she felt silly asking, but it was bothering her. "How old are you, Trace?"

"Twenty-six. Why?" He gave her a long side-eye, and Kylie wondered if he thought she was checking to see if he was too old for her. He definitely wasn't.

"Just wondering." Seeing him being so playful with his younger sister had made her curious.

"Okay. Well, you about to head in or what?"

Kylie's entire body flashed hot. "Yeah. Sorry. Going now." She turned so quickly she knocked into a guitar that had been precariously propped on the wall near the door. She bent down to catch it, made sure it was steady, and stood up to leave.

"Wait," he demanded, rooting her where she stood. Kylie looked down to check and see if the guitar was about to fall again. It wasn't.

"Yeah?" She turned slowly, uncertain of what he could possibly be about to say to her.

"You wanna to go to a party? With me? After the show?" Trace cleared his throat and she saw the thick knot in his neck move as he swallowed hard. Well, this was new. He seemed...nervous.

"Um, not sure I should be going to any more parties after—"

"It won't be like that. But it's totally fine if you have other plans."

Kylie rolled her eyes. "No, no plans. And yes, I'll go, as long as you promise to let me walk out on my own two feet." On her way out she could hear him laughing.

"I'm not making any promises," he hollered out after her.

chapter SIXTEEN

AFTER her set, she stuck around to watch Trace perform. She snagged a beer from the green room, hoping it would calm her nerves about the party afterwards. But watching the man on stage just got them all jangled up again. Pauly sat with her, but he rarely looked up from his phone. Kylie, however, couldn't take her eyes off the stage.

When Trace was on, when he really gave it his all, it was like no concert she'd ever been to. Kind of like jumping on a runaway freight train driven by a conductor with Attention Deficit Disorder.

She watched as he gave a melodramatic little spiel about a new song he was nervous to try and pleaded with the audience to bear with him. Then he began playing the piano and belting out a popular boy band song, poorly mimicking the high notes on purpose. Kylie laughed in spite of herself. Next he sang one of his own hits, followed by a cover of an Adele song that nearly blew her and the entire audience out of their seats.

Damn, the boy could sing. And Lord, those jeans. *Oh no.* She was becoming a Trace Corbin fangirl. She could feel it happening and she was powerless to stop it.

She was busy mentally punching herself in the face repeatedly when she saw Trace's little sister making her way over, his older sister not far behind.

"Kylie!" Rae squealed, hugging her like they were old friends. It made her miss Lulu even more than usual.

She barely had time to respond before the girl launched into a complicated story about how she'd seen The Rum Room video online and how she'd shown all of her friends. The girl barely took a breath. *Cheerleader*, Kylie thought. *Definitely a cheerleader.* Not that she didn't enjoy the high-spirited girl's open kindness. But if they'd gone to high school together, Kylie knew they certainly wouldn't have run in the same circles.

"So you're coming tonight, right?" Rae asked, catching her off guard. "To the party?"

"Way to put her on the spot, Rae," Claire Ann said, shooting Kylie an apologetic smile.

"Uh, yeah. Yeah, I am." Rae's answering smile was so big and open, Kylie smiled back. She knew the girl was probably only a year or two younger than her, but she felt like they were at least a decade apart.

"With Trace? Like, as his date?" Rae pressed.

"Rae," her sister warned.

"I was just asking," the younger girl said, a gleam twinkling in her eye.

Kylie fought off a smile. "He just asked if I'd come. I said I would." There. That was the truth.

"Cool. I'm so excited! I can't wait to tell all of my friends and oh, you'll get to meet some of them! But ignore Deidre. She's got issues about Trace but he's never really—"

"That's enough, Rae. Keep talking and she won't come," Claire Ann interrupted, practically dragging the younger girl away.

"See you tonight, Kylie! Great show by the way!" Rae called out as she was pulled onto the dance floor.

She just smiled and shook her head. A loud cough from beside her reminded Kylie that Pauly was still sitting in the booth with her. "So, you're going to a party with Trace? You sure that's a good idea?" he asked. But Kylie heard what he wasn't saying. *Do not go to a party with Trace. It's not a good idea.*

"Um, yeah. I guess so. I told him I would."

Pauly shifted in his seat and leaned closer to her. For a minute he didn't say anything as they both watched Trace on stage. He was singing a love song to some girl he'd pulled up on stage. It was Kylie's favorite song of his. *Goodbye in Your Eyes*. Reminded her of her dad. The last time she'd seen him.

She'd been eating breakfast at the kitchen table the morning he'd gone to work for the last time. The night before she'd had an argument with Darla that he'd tried to settle to keep the peace. She couldn't even remember what the fight was about, but she felt like he'd taken Darla's side and she'd told him so. Just before she'd slammed her bedroom door in his face.

That morning she ignored him because she was still hurting. Before he left for work he stopped, leaned down over her shoulder, and whispered, "You know you'll always be my best girl," in her ear before he kissed her on the top of the head and left. Forever.

Words she should've said were still jammed in her throat. She closed her eyes and tried to breathe. No use having a breakdown in front of Pauly.

"You okay, kid?" he asked, bringing her back to the present.

She nodded.

"Hey, I didn't mean to upset you, I just…look, Trace is not a bad guy, and typically I stay out of his personal life as much as I possibly can but…" Pauly ran a hand over his face and stared at her for a second. "I don't think it's a good idea for you to get involved with him right now," he began. She opened her mouth to tell the man he was way off, but he held up a hand. "Hear me out."

She sat back and waited.

"If you want to be *Kylie Ryans*, country music artist who gets taken seriously, it would be…unwise to align yourself with an already established artist in any way other than professionally. Trust me, I've seen it happen. Now, if you want to be Kylie Ryans, Trace Corbin's little sideshow fling, then by all means, party it up." Pauly leaned back to signal he'd said his piece.

She didn't miss the way he'd said her name each time. The first time had been with reverence. The second had been with contempt.

"You understand what I'm saying?" he asked.

"Yeah," she choked out. "Got it." No way she could go to a party with Trace and not risk losing Pauly's respect and probably any shot at having him manager her. But watching Trace onstage, she wanted to go. Badly. That, combined with the excitement so clear on Rae's face, and the thought of letting the girl down when she didn't show, made it even harder to imagine backing out. Even though she had to.

KYLIE stood naked on the bus. Trace still hadn't come back on from the bar, even though she was pretty sure his set had ended.

She stared into her closet. Pajamas. She should put on pajamas and tell Trace she wasn't feeling so hot and was just going to call it a night.

But her "I rode the bull at Bud's" tank top caught her eye and she remembered the perfect fit of those designer jeans from her last show. If she *were* going to the party, that's what she would wear. With her perfectly worn in cowgirl boots. And she'd take her hair down and just let it be wild. Maybe she'd dance with Trace a time or two, if it was that kind of party. Not that she was going. She wasn't. But a girl could fantasize, couldn't she?

Lulu would strangle her if she knew Kylie was about to turn down Trace's invitation. *You only get one shot at life,* she could practically hear her friend saying. Yeah, but she didn't want to ruin that life for one night of drunken stupidity. But those jeans and that smile, and he was just so... *male.* It would probably be worth it.

No. If this didn't work out, she had nothing to go back to. Nothing.

Well...that wasn't entirely true. Clive had said she would always be welcome back at The Rum Room. Right, 'cause waiting tables and cleaning hospitality rooms wouldn't seem like a nightmare compared to this.

Jammies it is. Just as she grabbed some sweats from the narrow wooden dresser, she heard voices. Trace was back.

A loud rapping on her door nearly gave her a heart attack.

"Kylie Lou, you ready?"

How on earth does he know my middle name? It wasn't exactly something she went around telling people. It had been her grandfather's name on her mom's side. He had passed away a week before she was born.

"Um, yeah, about the party—"

"You backing out on me?" The hurt in his voice nearly eviscerated her.

"No, I was just trying to decide what I should wear." *And if there's any way I can still manage to have a career after tonight.*

Trace's laughter made her feel better and worse. "Just throw on whatever. My family won't care. But we need to get goin'. Getting out of the parking lot is going to be a nightmare."

"Um, are we taking the bus?" Kylie wondered out loud as she pulled on her jeans and nearly toppled over.

"Definitely not." She heard a muffled laugh from the other side of the door. "I got us a ride, but we gotta get moving."

"'Kay." Kylie glanced at herself in the mirror one last time after she'd pulled her tank top over her head. *You are officially an idiot.*

THE ride Trace had gotten them was a pickup similar to the one her dad had driven. A buddy of his from home had loaned it out for the night. The interior smelled like mint Skoal and some type of men's cologne not nearly as expensive as Trace's.

Kylie had seen the disappointment in Pauly's eyes as she'd passed him on her way out. *Well, if I'm going to ruin my career before it even starts, might as well make it worth it.* She scooted a little closer to Trace on the bench seat.

He looked over and smiled. "Thanks for coming tonight. My family can be a little…much."

"No problem," Kylie said, suddenly feeling shy. "Thanks for inviting me."

Trace cleared his throat. Twice. "Um, actually Rae invited you."

She scooted back towards the door on her side. "Remind me to thank her then." She stared out the window as they twisted and turned down never-ending back roads. It seemed like they had been driving forever when Trace turned down a long dirt drive lined by a white fence. At least eighty acres spread out before them.

"Is this where you grew up?" Kylie asked, barely able to contain her astonishment.

"No, I wish. This is the house I bought after the first album went platinum. Claire Ann lives here now since I'm always on the road. Rae is pretty much her permanent houseguest."

"Ah."

Trace pulled the truck around to an enormous red barn behind the main house. At least twenty cars and trucks were already parked there. After putting the truck in park and shutting off the engine, he turned, causing the leather seat to protest beneath him. "Look, Kylie, I should probably warn you—"

Before he could finish his warning Rae tapped on Kylie's window, sending her jumping towards Trace. "Come on! You're late!" the perky little pixie shouted through the glass.

Kylie looked up at Trace. He just closed his eyes and shook his head.

She couldn't help but laugh. Rae was clearly a thorn in his side, but she adored him and he her. It kind of made her wish for a sibling. Rae knocked again, louder this time. Or not.

As soon as they stepped into the barn, a three-tier cake was produced. Every guest broke into a happy birthday flash mob.

Trace leaned down to whisper in Kylie's ear. "Sorry about this."

The heat of his breath made her shiver. It was his birthday. She hadn't known and hadn't brought a gift. That's why he'd looked so suspicious when she'd asked his age. He was twenty-six, *today*. Kylie didn't miss the fact that every other female guest was decked out in short dresses and boots or that they were sizing her up. She was pretty sure the "Deidre" Rae had mentioned was the busty blonde across the room giving her the death glare from hell. So she winked at her.

"Trace, I didn't know. I didn't get you a gift," she whispered up at him.

"Oh, yeah you did. You're making Rae's night," he said, nodding at the girl who was practically bouncing up and down.

"Happy birthday dear *TRACEY*," Kylie heard Rae belting over everyone. She raised an eyebrow at him. He shook his head and grinned. So that's why he went by Trace or Tray. This was interesting information.

As she was smiling at the crooners, Trace leaned down and whispered in her ear again. "My birthday was actually a few months ago, but Rae's is coming up and they had the decorations so they wanted to celebrate while I was in town."

"Ah," she said, still grinning and glancing at the white paper lanterns lit like stars above them. It was sweet that his sisters would go all out like this. Must be nice to be so cherished. Their love for their brother was practically radiating from both of their faces as Trace blew out his candles. She recognized the expression. It was the same way her daddy used to look at her.

chapter SEVENTEEN

RAE spent most of the night dragging Kylie around and introducing her to people. Aunts, uncles, cousins, friends from high school, writing buddies, and drinking buddies. It seemed like everyone Trace knew was there. Conspicuously absent were his parents.

When she and Rae stepped out for some air, Kylie asked her where they were tonight. When she saw the pain and discomfort on the girl's face, she wished she hadn't.

"If Trace hasn't mentioned them, he'd probably rather I didn't," she said quietly, glancing back towards the barn.

"Oh, okay. Well in that case—"

"But he'll probably never mention it."

"I shouldn't have asked. Sorry, I was just—"

Rae waved her hand as if it wasn't a big deal. "My dad was a musician. He was all about making it big in country music. As kids, he and his brothers sang in church and were even on the radio. But as he got older, things just didn't work out. He never could let it go. He drank. A lot. He was violent when he was drunk." Rae shuddered visibly and Kylie noticed how thin and frail the usually vibrant girl suddenly seemed. "Trace made sure none of that ever reached me, and he did his best to protect Claire Ann, but my mom wouldn't stay out of my dad's path."

"Oh God, Rae. I'm so sorry." She hated herself even more for prying. This was totally none of her business.

"It's okay. It was a long time ago and I don't remember it all that well," she assured Kylie with a shrug. "My dad died of colon cancer when I was ten and Trace was twenty. Finally free of having to protect us all, he wanted to go to Nashville and cut a record with some guys he was in a band with."

Well this was new. Kylie had never heard of Trace being in a band.

Even in the dark, she could tell that Trace's little sister was nervous about what she was about to reveal. But the girl bit her lip and continued. "My mom totally freaked. I'm talking *ballistic*. She said if he followed in Dad's footsteps he would be dead to her."

"What?" Kylie couldn't even comprehend a mother not being proud of having a famous son.

"Yeah. They, um, still don't talk. She won't even say his name and we can't say it around her," Rae finished softly. The sadness in her voice made Kylie feel hollowed out inside.

"But he made it, and he's not like his dad at all, right?"

Trace's sister was quiet for a long time. The silence stretched out between them and Kylie thought of Trace's drinking. Him missing concerts, the things she'd seen in tabloids and on TMZ, him stumbling in and out of cabs, punching out cameramen, what had happened with Steven Blythe, and then the most recent incident in Jackson. Ah.

"But it's not like..." Kylie trailed off, unsure of how much Rae knew or should know.

The difference was, the only person Trace really hurt was himself.

Knowing what she did now, the dark horrified look she'd seen in his eyes in Jackson, when he'd grabbed her made so much more sense. His walking away from her that night in Mobile did too. She ran a hand through her hair and struggled to stay put. She wanted to see Trace. And she kind of didn't want to. Because she wanted to wrap her arms around him, kiss him, and tell him how sorry she was about his dad and his mom and how unfair life was. That it was okay and she understood. But he wouldn't want her pity, just like she hadn't wanted anyone's when her dad died.

"We should get back," Rae said, tilting her head towards the barn and jolting Kylie from her thoughts. "And hey, please don't tell Trace I told you about all our family drama."

Kylie nodded. "Of course not." She linked her arm in Rae's and they headed back into the party.

Once she was back in the barn, Kylie chatted with a few people about her music and with Claire Ann about what a force of nature Rae was.

"How's he doing?" Claire Ann asked barely loud enough to be heard, keeping her eyes across the room on Trace. Kylie saw him smiling and laughing with his buddies, and she could hardly imagine him as a kid protecting his sisters from a violent drunk of a father. But the way he'd reacted with Steven…it made sense now, and yeah, she could see it because she had.

"Good, mostly. There was the one thing in Dallas but other than that…" Kylie really wanted to tell the woman that she didn't know how he was because they really weren't close like that. He'd been avoiding her just as much as she was keeping her distance from him. In fact, if it wasn't for Rae, she was pretty sure she wouldn't even be here.

"Good," Claire Ann said with a relieved smile. "He's a good man, even if he doesn't always act like one."

"I can see that," Kylie answered softly. As if he could tell they were talking about him, Trace turned and met her gaze. She flushed with embarrassment and looked away.

By the time she looked back in his direction, he was barely a foot away. "Not gossipin' about me over here, are you, Claire Ann?"

"Me? Never. I leave that to Rae," she answered with a grin.

"Uh huh," he murmured, eyeing both of them suspiciously. "So, you had enough yet? Ready to get back to home sweet bus?" he asked, turning to face Kylie.

"I don't want to take you away from your party. I can get a cab back in a little while," she told him.

"I don't think so, darlin'. First of all, there aren't exactly a ton of cabs out here, and second, what kind of man brings a girl to a party and doesn't make sure she gets home safe?"

Kylie couldn't respond right away. The way he'd called her darlin' didn't seem like the generic way most southern guys said it. It was warm and his voice melted around it like he meant it. God, she had to get out of here. She was totally losing her grip on reality.

"You're not staying the night here?" Claire Ann spoke up before Kylie could say anything. "Rae will be crushed."

"Aw hell, don't do that, Claire Ann. It's bad enough Rae guilted her in to coming to this," Trace whined as he gestured to the party. "But now you guys are going to turn it in to a sleepover?"

"Hey, you do what you want," his sister began, holding her hands up. "You can be the one to tell Rae you're leaving to go sleep on a bus." She winked at Kylie and disappeared into the crowd.

"We don't have to leave for South Carolina until tomorrow night. I kind of thought Pauly was going to get us a hotel anyways," Kylie said quietly, not wanting to intrude.

"Yeah, he was, or he did." Trace shrugged. "But there are several guest rooms and I do make one hell of an omelet," he said, barely containing his boyish grin.

"Well, I hardly ever turn down food and now I have to know if you're as good as you say."

"Always darlin'. Always." Trace's cocky exterior had returned, but now it was sexier and less irritating than before.

"Slumber party it is then," she said with exaggerated enthusiasm. Trace gave her a goofy two thumbs up and she couldn't help but feel happy that she'd made him happy.

When he pulled her onto the dance floor, she didn't resist. Dancing with Trace made her feel alive and she loved watching him laugh easily as they talked and joked. The closer he held her, the tighter she wanted to be held.

"I'm glad you came," he said softly to the top of her head.

"Me too," she mumbled back.

"You've been avoiding me." It wasn't a question. And it was the truth. So Kylie said nothing. "Probably a good idea." The sadness in his voice sent a pang of guilt through her.

"You pretty much told me to," she whispered.

"I did. And I meant it. I'm not that guy, Kylie."

"What guy?" she asked, pulling back to look at his face so she could figure out what in the world he was talking about.

"That guy you deserve. The one who would take you on dates, write you love songs, serenade you in public, send you flowers, and all that shit. That's not me. I don't do relationships."

"So I noticed." Sighing loudly, she pulled him back to her. Who the hell ever said she needed all of those things? She was pretty damn happy right where she was. "Can I ask why?"

"Why, what?"

"Why you don't do relationships."

Not that she necessarily wanted one. She had a career to think about, even if she was tanking it with everything she had at this particular moment.

"Because I let people down," Trace said evenly before clearing his throat.

"So don't."

A deep laugh from her dance partner made her smile. "I'm working on it, Kylie Lou."

"That's good enough for me." She shrugged and leaned her head on his warm shoulder. God, he smelled good. She wanted to breathe him in until it hurt, but didn't want to show him all her crazy when they were finally getting along.

"You really ride the bull at Bud's?" Trace asked, smoothly switching the subject to something lighter.

"Hell yeah I did," Kylie answered. Like she'd wear the shirt if she hadn't.

"How long did you last?'

She grinned up at him. "I rode the full eight. That's how I got the shirt."

Another throaty laugh, but this one had a nervous edge to it. "Bet you're one hell of a rider."

Goosebumps broke out over her skin and she barely stifled a shiver. "Only one way to find out. Not sure you could handle it though, old man."

Clutching her tighter, Trace licked his lips so close to her face she could feel the wet warmth of his tongue. "There are a lot of beds in that house, darlin'. I'd behave myself if I were you."

"I'll take that under advisement."

chapter EIGHTEEN

KYLIE woke up in Trace's bed feeling more rested than she probably ever had in her entire life. Rain pretty much ended the party around three in the morning, and Rae had loaned her some pajamas.

Between that and Trace insisting that she sleep in the master bedroom while he took a guest room, she was almost too cozy for comfort. This was the kind of bed she could spend an entire afternoon in. Longer if a certain someone joined her. His sheets smelled like him and she didn't want to shower for fear she'd wash his scent off. And yes, she realized exactly how pathetic that was.

Intoxicating aromas of bacon and coffee wafted to her and she felt like she could float to the kitchen following her nose. She resisted and freshened up in the bathroom first, throwing on her jeans and tank top from the night before. She borrowed a dark blue plaid button up from Trace's closet and threw it on over her tank. Man, the boy loved his plaid.

Following the sound of voices chattering into the kitchen, she found Rae sitting at an enormous oak table while Claire Ann was grabbing dishes from a cabinet. Trace was at the stove, shirtless in dark sweats. Kylie's mouth watered and she prayed it was because of the food.

The table was literally crammed full with bacon, sausage, omelets, and a basket of biscuits with a full gravy boat next to it. A bowl of sliced fruit sat in the middle. Had Trace cooked all of this? If so, Kylie was going to give up her singing career and ask him to marry her. *Not funny. Do not even go there.*

"Morning," she said quietly, interrupting Rae and Trace's debate on bacon versus sausage.

Everyone stopped and stared at her for a second. Trace flinched like he'd been popped with grease. Well, that was what he got for cooking shirtless.

"Good morning, sleepyhead," Rae chimed, sending everyone back into action.

Trace shook his head and went back to cooking. "Western omelets on the left, Kylie. Plain cheese on your right," he called over to her.

Kylie took her cue from everyone else and just started loading her plate. She chose a western omelet, two pieces of bacon, and a giant biscuit. She grabbed a few pieces of fruit just to make herself feel better about the greasy goodness on her plate.

"Juice or coffee?" Claire Ann asked her.

"Both sound good. I'll take coffee, please. Black with sugar."

After everyone was seated at the table, Claire Ann said a quick blessing over the food. Kylie was fine until the woman added a part at the end about being thankful for having Trace and Kylie home. At that, her world shifted, titling Kylie so hard she had to grip the table to keep from falling out into the floor. She couldn't even swallow her perfect bite of cheesy meaty deliciousness that was her omelet. This wasn't her home—she didn't need to dare think of it that way. This wasn't even her family. She had no family. The laughter, the smiles, the friendly teasing, the food—this wasn't for her. This would never be her life. She'd buried the closest thing she'd ever have to this along with her dad.

"Um, excuse me a second," she said, standing abruptly. Before anyone could stop her, she bolted back towards Trace's room.

Inexplicable tears formed in her eyes and a giant knot wedged itself in her throat. What a stupid idea this was. *Breathe, Kylie. Just get through breakfast, do this last show in South Carolina, and do not ever go near Trace Corbin or anyone related to him ever again.*

And then it hit her. This was it, the last show. And it was tomorrow night. The tears behind Kylie's eyes spilled down her cheeks. She darted in the bathroom to grab some tissue. Somehow it felt like the beginning even though it was the end. She had to keep reminding herself of that. It was the end of this tour. But maybe the beginning of her career? Her hands shook as she wiped her tears. What the hell was she so upset about?

"Kylie, you all right in there?" Trace's voice came from outside the bedroom.

She swallowed hard. Nope, no way she could talk without him hearing the tremors in her voice.

"Mmhm," she tried to mumble loud enough for him to hear.

"What?" King of impatience that he was, he pushed the bedroom door open. She thought briefly about pulling the bathroom door closed to keep him from seeing her, but that just seemed overly dramatic and childish. Kind of like crying before you've even had breakfast.

"Hey," he said softly, stepping closer as he took in her emotional meltdown. "What's the matter, baby?" Even Trace startled at his words. "Kylie, I meant to say Kylie. I have sisters so when women cry, I get all—" He didn't finish his sentence, just waved his hand around to indicate that he was a little scattered. She understood the feeling.

"Nothing. It's nothing. I'm fine." She tried to smile, but this was pretty much the most humiliating situation she'd ever been in. Well, one of them.

"Yeah, you look like you're feeling super fine," he said, crossing his arms over his bare chest and leaning against the bathroom counter. "And do not even say it was my cooking because you didn't even eat anything."

Kylie laughed quietly and shook her head. "Family stuff," she choked out.

"Ah." For a moment neither of them said anything. Then Trace reached over and wiped a tear from her cheek. When he used that same hand to tuck a stray strand of her hair behind her ear, it nearly broke her apart all over again. Her mind struggled to reconcile this man, the one who cooked, wiped tears, and protected his sisters, with the selfish ass she'd seen on the bus.

"Tell you what," he began, taking a step back. "Lay back down. I'll tell them you aren't feeling well and I'll bring you breakfast in bed." His words were another jolt to Kylie's bruised heart.

"Why would you do that?" she asked, swiping her nose with his shirtsleeve.

"Because, under all these muscles is a halfway decent guy. And this was a lot to throw on you when you thought you were just coming to a party."

It sounded like heaven on earth, but Kylie worried what his sisters would think of her. She didn't want to look like some spoiled brat. She liked them. She had a good time talking with both of them last night. That was the problem. She really liked all of them. And this down home version of Trace. Too much. Way, way too much.

"Okay?" Trace probed.

She nodded and he clapped his hands together. "All right then." And then he was gone. Suddenly Kylie felt drained and utterly exhausted. Maybe she needed more rest. Or coffee. Or both.

Slipping her jeans off and placing them on the nightstand, she started to get back in the bed. She planned to snuggle in and pull the covers up to her waist before Trace returned. But he was like The frickin' Flash.

"Okay, I brought, um whoa—"

Kylie jumped into the bed and then burst into laughter at his panicked expression. The shirt was past her thighs and he was Captain Panty Dropper of country music. Surely he wasn't as embarrassed as he looked.

"I bring you breakfast in bed, you flash me, then laugh at me. Nice."

"I did not flash you, at least not on purpose." Kylie laughed harder, relieved that the awkward tension from her crying jag in the bathroom seemed to be gone.

"Yeah well, you can keep that shirt by the way. Pretty sure I'll never be able to look at it the same again," he said, putting the tray with her breakfast on the bed. She noticed he'd added to her plate.

"Aw, but then you won't have anything to remember me by," she teased, enjoying the light flirty atmosphere.

Trace's face was serious as he sat her coffee and a cup of orange juice on the night table next to her jeans. "Kylie, you sang the hell out of my song the first time I laid eyes on you and then you tore into me with the fury of ten hells the first time we ever actually spoke. After what happened in Jackson…" He closed his eyes and swallowed hard before he finished. "I don't think I'll be forgetting you anytime soon." When he opened them, his usually bright eyes were dark and hooded as they burned into hers.

"Okay," she said, taking a bite of omelet and chewing carefully before swallowing. It was still warm, making her to wonder if he'd reheated it. "I'll keep the shirt then."

Trace held her captive in his gaze for a few more seconds and then he stood abruptly. "Finish your breakfast and get cleaned up. I'll give you the grand tour of the property and then we can head back to the bus."

"Pauly's probably mad at me," she said quietly. *Or at least he will be when he notices me gawking at you like I love you.*

"He'll get over it," Trace answered with a smirk.

Yeah, but will I?

chapter NINETEEN

After finishing her breakfast, Kylie found Trace out back sitting in a golf cart.

"Nice," she commented as she stepped carefully around the ashes of the previous night's bonfire.

"Yeah, I try to ride in style wherever I go," he said with a grin.

The property was huge. And beautiful. Kylie could only imagine what it would look like in the fall.

"When I get some time off I plan to get a few horses, maybe breed paints or something."

"My grandparents had a few quarter horses. They were retired racers, just used them for riding lessons, kid's birthday parties, stuff like that," Kylie told him. An emotion she was getting used to swept over her. Loss.

Thankfully Trace didn't ask any questions. After they'd ridden too far to see the house, he pulled the golf cart over near a brown fence that probably could've used a new paint job.

"It gets kind of hilly from here on out. The ol' cart's not really ready for off-roading yet."

"Yet?" she asked with a raised brow.

Trace grinned and the mischievous gleam in his eye told her he had actual plans for jacking up that golf cart. Artist of the Year or not, he was still such a boy. Kylie remembered her conversation with Rae. According to his little sister, he'd never really gotten to be a kid or a teenager. No wonder he acted like he was still fifteen. He'd had to act like he was thirty-five the first time around.

They walked for a few minutes, hands barely grazing as they passed. Trace didn't seem to notice but each brush of bare skin sent a shiver of electricity humming through Kylie's body.

"Here we are," he told her as they reached a small shed. "Careful, it's still muddy from the rain last night."

Trace took her hand and Kylie's heart stuttered and then took off as if it were trying to escape her chest. He didn't let go until they reached the door to the shed and he had to retrieve keys from his pocket to unlock it.

The lights flickered on when they stepped inside and Kylie realized it wasn't a shed at all. It was a small recording studio. Cozy dark furniture filled a small living area that opened into a tiny kitchenette. A stone fireplace tucked into the corner smelled lightly of ash.

"The writing room," Trace said gesturing to the couches. She noticed they faced a wall made entirely of glass so the breathtaking view of the property was still visible. He led her into a soundproof room that had some exposed wiring. "Still working on this part," he told her. "There's a bathroom back there with a shower, too."

Kylie nodded. "So when this tour's over and I'm out of a job, I think I might just sneak in here and live."

Trace's head fell back as he laughed.

"I'm only half kidding," she said, glaring at him. "Don't be surprised if you find me crashed out on your couch next time you come home."

"I could probably live with that," he said, all hints of humor gone from his voice. The silence stretched out and Kylie tried to think of something light and funny to say. Things were taking a turn towards awkwardsville.

"Promise not to dump any liquor I find, and I'll replace any beer I drink." She winked to let him know she was over it.

"Damn right," he growled, nudging an elbow into her ribs, making her laugh out loud. The strained muscles in her stomach loosened a bit.

"You working on something?" she asked, lifting a hand to point at a notebook on the coffee table once they were back in the living room.

"Sort of. Not really. Actually I came out here late last night and jotted some stuff down." His face pinked with something that looked like embarrassment.

She could understand how being home would trigger an urge to write.

"Can I take a look?" She stepped towards the table but stopped when she saw Trace's shoulder's go stiff.

"Never mind, sorry," she mumbled, remembering how she flipped out on the bus when he looked at her writing.

"No, it's cool. I just don't really…it's just not actually a song yet." Trace shrugged and handed her the notebook. She lowered herself onto the couch behind her and started skimming the lines he'd written. And she could hear it. In fact, it almost made her wonder if he'd read the song she'd started writing about him. No, that wasn't possible. She'd made sure he was never alone with her book again once she'd added those lines.

While she was looking at the words Trace had scrawled across the pages, he picked up a guitar and started playing bits and pieces of songs she recognized. One of his, one of hers. Some she could tell he was still trying to work out. When he strummed out a melody that was damn near exactly what she was hearing in her head, she called out in excited panic.

"Wait! Go back," she told him, looking up at his eyes. He looked almost drugged. *Playing out here alone makes him happy.* Her heart gave a little squeeze at the realization.

"What?" Trace startled.

"Go back and play those last few chords again, but a little slower."

"Yes, boss."

Softly, practically under her breath, she began singing his lyrics, adding a few of her own here and there.

Suddenly Trace stopped playing. "Here," he said, handing her a pen. "Write down those last two lines." She didn't want to tell him that it wasn't necessary, that she had them memorized. She'd written them down in a notebook that was tucked away under her mattress on the bus.

Taking the pen he offered, she jotted down the lines she'd added.

Seeing their lyrics mingling together on the page was doing something to her that made her nervous. Each stroke of ink on the paper felt like a caress of Trace's skin. When a line of one of her letters crossed into his, she felt like she was pressing herself against him.

"Um, maybe we should take a break," she said, making more than a serious effort to control her breathing.

"No way, you're in the zone. Let me see what you have," he said, reaching for the notebook. Kylie would've felt more comfortable handing him a naked picture of herself.

Okay, maybe not *more* comfortable, but about as exposed.

Big blue eyes, and a pretty little smile, that's what everyone else sees, he began as he strummed along. God, he was singing her part. Her words. And wow, he could seriously sing. His vocal skills were even more impressive in private. Kylie realized she was holding her breath and tried to exhale without being obvious.

They think I'm pink champagne, you know I'm whiskey and rage. They want love songs and romance, you know I'm get drunk and let's dance. I try and I try, to live their lies, be what they need me to be. But you know the truth. Know I'm all scarred and bruised, on the other side of me.

The music stopped and Kylie couldn't bring herself to look at the man across from her.

When she finally risked a glance, he wasn't even looking at her. He was jotting something down in the notebook. She watched as he gripped the guitar and began again. *Big strong man, singin' lead in the band, that's what everyone else sees. They think I'm bulls and beers, you know I'm pain and fears. They want singin' and drinkin,' you know I'm drownin' and sinkin.'*

Trace paused and made a few marks with his pen before continuing on.

But I'll keep it all in, hide it under a grin. Cause you're the only one who sees, the other side of me.

Kylie knew the next few lines by heart so she sang along. *The world wants fun and shiny and new, but I save the best of me for when I'm alone with you. Yeah I'll keep it all in, hide it under a grin. 'Cause you're the only one who sees, yeah you're the only one who sees, the other side of me.*

For a moment they both just stared at each other, the residual intensity of their music swirling in the air, making it thick between them. It was rough and raw, and the chord progression needed work, but it had potential. Kylie's face began to tingle, along with some other parts of her anatomy. The space between them surged with electricity that had a voltage so high it would turn the first one who entered into ash.

She knew she should be the first to look away, but she couldn't. *This is it*, she thought to herself. *No turning back now*. Not that she wanted to. Trace's eyes conveyed the same want she knew hers did. For a moment. Then he shook his head as if clearing the lust from it. He rubbed the back of his neck and looked away from her.

"Well, that was unexpected," he said as he propped the guitar against the couch and cleared his throat. "Maybe when we both have some time we could try and write together, maybe record something."

"Maybe," Kylie said. She lifted her shoulder in what she hoped was a noncommittal shrug. That was what Pauly had been wanting all along—she'd heard him on the phone enough to know that. Somehow writing and singing with Trace felt dangerous. Like she might enjoy it a little too much, get carried away and reveal more than she wanted to. Like the fact that she really wanted him to kiss her, hard and deep, just to know what it would feel like.

chapter TWENTY

BEFORE they left, Kylie took one last look at the writing room. She wanted to memorize it so she could recall that experience whenever she wanted. It was like riding a roller coaster. The whole time it was happening she was thinking, *This is crazy. What am I doing*? But when it was over, she'd have given anything to do it again.

The buzzing of Trace's phone interrupted her thoughts. He pulled it from his shirt pocket and looked at the screen before tucking it back away quickly. "Text from Rae. The girls are going shopping. They said it was nice meeting you and they hope you'll come back and visit." Something about the look on his face told Kylie that his little sister's text had said more than that, but she didn't want to pry.

"I'd like that, especially since I made such an ass out of myself this morning." She could feel her skin flashing hot just thinking about it.

"Nah, I told them you weren't feeling well. Rae kind of thinks you're pregnant and she might post it on her Facepage but other than that, no big."

Slapping Trace on the arm she told him, "It's Facebook genius, but that's real funny."

For a minute he just looked at her with a goofy grin on his face, but then his expression softened into something serious. "Want to tell me what was up this morning? Or you can tell me to mind my own damn business. Whichever," he told her with a shrug as they leaned against the fence.

Kylie propped a boot on the golf cart and looked at Trace. It was one more show and then she'd probably never see him again. What the hell.

She took a deep breath and tried to put her thoughts into words. Putting them into lyrics came so much more easily. "My dad was pretty much all the family I had left. He was killed in an accident at the factory where he worked right before last Christmas. I was eating breakfast the last time I saw him alive." Kylie swallowed hard. There was more, but she wasn't sure she could get it out. "The factory said the accident was a result of something he failed to do, gross negligence they called it, so they didn't pay any kind of…whatever it's called. His small life insurance policy paid for the funeral and the burial, but I can't afford a headstone yet. When this tour ends tomorrow, I will be completely one hundred percent on my own. I was actually starting to be okay with it until…" There was no way to describe what she felt.

"Until this morning when you saw my big happy family having breakfast?" Trace finished for her, tilting his head in her direction.

"No, it wasn't like that. It was just…" *I wanted to pretend they were mine. That you were mine.*

"Well, if it makes you feel any better, we weren't always so happy," he said barely loud enough for her to hear.

"No, of course that doesn't make me feel better. But yeah, Rae mentioned something about that." Kylie's gut twisted. She hoped she wasn't getting the girl in trouble.

"Of course she did," he said through clenched teeth.

Kylie's hand reached out and landed on Trace's arm without her permission. "Don't be mad. She was just trying to explain why…"

"Why I'm such an ass?" Trace offered.

"Something like that," she answered with a smile, grateful he didn't seem too angry with his little sister.

"Can I ask where your mom is?"

"In Heaven with my dad, I hope," she whispered, then cleared her throat. "She died in a car accident on her way to work when I was almost two. She'd already dropped me off at daycare. I don't really remember much about her."

"I'm sorry to hear that."

She could hear the tightness in his voice, and wondered if he was thinking of his own mom. Feeling guilty for knowing so much about his situation without him having volunteered it, made her want to let him in on more than she normally would have.

"It was actually okay being raised by my dad. We went hunting and fishing a lot, rode four-wheelers, played baseball. He even took me to a few Oklahoma State football games."

"You like hunting, fishing, four-wheelers, and sports." Trace smiled a broad, heart-melting smile at her. "You're every guy's dream girl. Bet that was not your dad's intention."

Kylie laughed. "No, probably not." In fact, she was pretty sure that was exactly why he'd married Darla right before she'd turned thirteen. He was worried he was turning his little girl into a boy.

"Well, I'm sorry to hear about your parents. I don't keep in touch with my family like I should, to be honest. Surely you've seen how much drama some artists' families can cause." Kylie vaguely remembered hearing something about Trace's mom writing a tell-all book about him. She almost flinched at how much pain that must've caused, his mom disowning him and then cashing in like that. "Not that it's any consolation, but at least you don't have to deal with any of that. It's actually one of the reasons Pauly wanted you on the tour even though you were an unknown. You didn't come with any baggage."

"Um, yeah, lucky me."

"So…there's just no one?" Trace's eyes were full of compassion that Kylie didn't know if she wanted. Or deserved.

"Nope, just me."

"Well, I have somehow managed to ruin what was supposed to be a fun tour of the farm, so I'm feeling pretty good about myself right now."

She smiled up at him. "It's fine. Not like I'm going to have any secrets if Cora has anything to say about it." As soon as the words were out of her mouth, the bottom of Kylie's stomach gave out. She had one secret. And it was a pretty damn big one. But there was no reason to bring up Darla. That part of her life was over.

"Since I've already turned this into an episode of Dr. Phil, can I give you some advice?"

"Sure, as long as I don't have to actually take it." She bit her lip, hoping he would realize she was only half kidding.

"Course not," he told her with a wink. "It's just that it's come to my attention recently that you've actually got some talent, and I know how this industry can be…it's a machine, Kylie and it can churn and burn you into something you're not just as easily as it can toss you out on your ass if you don't give it what it needs. And what it needs is money, ticket sales, number one hits, radio play, and a brand. That's what they're going to turn you into—a brand. I'm not saying it's the worst thing in the world just…try not to forget who you actually are under all that."

It was the most she'd ever heard him say in the entire time they'd known each other. The look in his eyes was hard and intense and almost frightening. Like he was trying to will her to believe him with his glare. It also explained why he was so damn set on being late to sound check after the label had told him not to be. Sort of.

"This is happenin' a lot faster for you than it does for most people. Than it did for me." Trace cleared his throat and examined his hands. "In the beginning, pretty much everyone lied to me. Kept things from me. I had to figure out a lot of hard truths on my own." She swallowed hard as Trace's gaze faded to a different time. A strange and unfamiliar feeling of regret that she hadn't known him back them, hadn't been able to be there for him, tugged at her heart. "Just don't forget that you can say no, because if you change who you are for them, then Kylie didn't really make it—someone else did."

The silence pulled and strained between them. She could hear him breathing heavily. Or maybe it was her. "Now can I ask you something?" she asked, semi-hopeful that he would say no. He just nodded, his eyes moving from his hands to her eyes, then settling on the boot she was still resting against the hood of the golf cart. "Would you do anything differently? If you had it to do all over again, would you still have moved to Nashville?"

Trace's jaw twitched and she thought she saw him wince. *Nice, Kylie. Worst question ever.*

"I'D do some things differently, yeah, but I'd probably still have ended up in music one way or another," he finally answered, though he still didn't meet her eyes. "Music was my safe place growin' up," he continued. His thousand-yard stare told Kylie he wasn't seeing the acres of land spread out before him, but something else entirely. "When there was music in my house it meant things were good. Everyone was happy, dancing, laughing, just enjoying being alive. When the music stopped…" Trace's chest rose and fell as the grin he wore faded and she waited silently for him to finish. But he just shook his head as his eyes unglazed, returning him to the present. His skin held a slight flush and she wasn't sure if it was from the wind or the conversation.

Kylie let out the breath she hadn't realized she was holding. A breeze swirled past, sending loose blond strands of hair whipping into her face. "Rae said you were in a band when you first started out," she offered as she pushed the hair out of her eyes.

"Yeah. I was actually, with a couple of the guys that were at the party last night. But now they're all married with kids and real jobs, and I'm living on a bus."

Her mouth gaped open. She couldn't believe he was serious. "Trace... You have a real job, one I'm sure most of those guys would happily trade their nine-to-fives for."

He folded his arms across his chest before he spoke again. "Yeah, you're probably right. Sometimes I just feel like it's taking over my life." He paused for a moment and stared up at the sky, as if looking for an answer to a question Kylie didn't know had been asked. "No, it's more like I'm missing out on actually having a life because of it. Like you said, won't be much longer till someone else comes along and replaces me and I've given up...pretty much everything for this."

"You know I didn't mean that. I was angry," she reassured him. This was the first time she'd seem him let his guard down. It threw her off balance. Trying to comfort him and keep her own guard up at the same time was nearly impossible.

"Doesn't make it any less true. It's not like anyone really cares if I release another album or not—there are plenty of other guys out there singing similar stuff."

"I care," she told him, shrugging as if it wasn't difficult for her to admit.

"Hell, you don't even *like* me," he came back at her with a grin.

"What's that got to do with anything?" *Besides the fact that it's not true.*

"So tell me why you care if I keep recording or not," Trace challenged.

Kylie took a deep breath, hoping her answer would be coherent and not turn into some mushy overshare. "*Goodbye in Your Eyes* reminds me of my dad. Of the things I would've said if I'd known the last time I saw him would be the last time," she answered quietly, hoping the breeze would blow her words to wherever her dad was. When Trace didn't say anything she continued. "I was born at 5:38 in the morning, and every year he barged into my room with his guitar at exactly 5:38 singing *Happy Birthday*." Kylie paused to take a healing breath. "The line you wrote, '*Every time that time comes around, I feel your goodbye all over again*,' one of the best lines ever written as far as I'm concerned."

One side of Trace's mouth lifted before he spoke. "Up until now, I've pretty much had a smart ass remark for just about everything. You're the first woman I've ever met who can shut me up. It blows Pauly's mind," Trace told her with a light huff that sounded like soft laughter. "And mine," he finished.

"Yeah, well, I'm probably the only woman you've ever associated with that has a triple digit IQ." She bit her bottom lip and smiled to herself.

When Trace didn't respond, Kylie pushed up off the fence and stood straight.

"Kylie—" he began, but she cut him off.

"We should probably get back. I bet Pauly's freaking out," she said, mostly just to keep things from getting even more intense.

"Yeah, okay," he agreed.

As she turned to step into the golf cart, something wet thudded against her hip. She looked down. Mud was splattered on her jeans and the bottom corner of her shirt. Well, Trace's shirt. "What the hell?"

Trace returned her puzzled look with a wicked grin and raised eyebrows. "That's for insinuating I date bimbos," he informed her, pointing at her mud-soaked hip.

"Oh yeah?" Kylie scooped up a handful of mud and flung it at his chest. Direct hit. "Well *that's* for standing me up in Dallas."

As soon as the words were out of her mouth, another clump of mud splattered against her shoulder. "That's for going into The Player's Club and a bedroom with a complete stranger all in the same night."

"I was totally fine," she argued as she slung a handful of moist earth that nailed her target a lot closer to his crotch than she'd meant to. "That's for carrying me out like a cave man."

"Oh, I'll show you cave man." Trace grunted as he ran towards her with two handfuls of black sludge.

Kylie squealed and ran, nearly tripping over her own feet as she tried to scoop up some more ammo. She'd always been a fast runner, but he was faster.

By the time the mud fight ended, they were both panting and caked head to toe with mud.

"No way you're riding in my golf cart like that," he told her, gesturing to her mud covered clothes.

"Oh yeah, what about you?"

Trace looked down at his drenched clothing. "I have to admit, you have much better aim than I would've guessed."

"Why, Mr. Corbin, was that a compliment?"

His head snapped up and he glared at her. "I told you not to call me that."

"Okay, *Tracey*."

He shook his head, sending droplets of muddy water dripping from his hair. "I could kill Rae sometimes, I swear. Seriously, you cannot go around calling me that. I mean it."

"And if I do?"

"Then I'll—" He didn't get to finish the threat because a giant clump of mud hit him square in the mouth.

He took off after her, chasing Kylie almost all the way back to the house, both of them deserting the golf cart. Grabbing her around the waist, he carried her kicking and screaming to the man-made pond Rae had told her he'd built himself.

"In you go," he said as he tossed her in.

"Trace, no! Please, I can't swim!" she screamed in mid-air. Trace splashed into the water right behind her. Just as he wrapped an arm around her waist to tow her out, she leapt up and dunked him under.

When he finally pushed her off of him and came up for air, she was laughing. Damn near hysterically. "You should've seen your face." Kylie cracked up, bobbing in the murky water.

"You," he said as he shook his wet hair in her direction, "are not a nice girl."

"Never said I was." She smirked at his back as he hoisted himself out onto the grass.

"Guess I should've figured that out when you dumped thirty thousand dollars worth of alcohol the drain," he muttered. Kylie winced at the amount—she hadn't realized it was so much. But then she laughed, thankful they were able to joke about it. "Truce?" he asked, reaching out his hand to help her out of the pond.

"Truce," she said, taking it. But she lost her footing as soon as he let go and she stumbled into his arms.

"Whoa, you okay?" his eyes met hers and she felt heat flood to places she knew she shouldn't be thinking about.

Please kiss me, she thought at him. But he either didn't get the message or he ignored it, because he released her as if she'd caught fire.

"I'm fine," she mumbled as the heavy weight of disappointment settled on her chest.

"We're going to have to strip these wet clothes off in the sunroom and shower before we head back."

At Trace's mention of removing clothing, Kylie's heart missed a beat and restarted all out of rhythm. "Um, I don't exactly have anything else to put on."

"Just grab something of Rae's and I'll throw our stuff in the wash," he said over his shoulder as he walked towards the house.

When they reached the sunroom, Trace was a perfect gentleman, much to her frustration. He handed her a towel, then did not so much as glance in her direction as he stripped down to his boxer briefs and wrapped a towel around his waist. She, on the other hand, couldn't get enough. The sight of his bare skin had her synapses firing like AK-47 rounds.

He was thick and muscular and had just a hint of a farmer's tan. Back muscles rippling with each movement reminded Kylie of the horses her grandparents had. Something clicked in her head as she realized what it was that had her practically panting after him. He was loaded, like probably obscenely wealthy, but he did all the work around the farm himself. Still took care of his sisters. Himself. Had callouses on his hands like her daddy did, because he wasn't afraid of hard work. Okay, and yeah, he was hot as hell and could sing a girl's panties right off of her.

She peeled her wet clothes off slowly, hoping he'd turn and look, but he just picked up what she'd dropped and darted out of the room. She kept her drenched bra and panties on and wrapped the towel around herself. She was feeling majorly insecure due to the not-at-all-interested vibe Trace was suddenly radiating in her direction.

She headed towards the master bedroom with the intention of using that bathroom to shower, but changed direction at the last minute. Since he was gone, she decided to go ahead and add her bra and panties to the laundry. Borrowing Rae's clothes was one thing, but the thought of wearing someone else's underwear freaked her out.

She padded barefoot back towards the sound of a whirring washing machine. Trace was still nowhere to been seen when she finally found the laundry room. She dropped her towel and tossed her bra in the machine. She had just begun to slide her underwear down when the sharp intake of breath alerted her to the broad frame that darkened the laundry room doorway.

chapter TWENTY TWO

JUST as she started to rush to cover herself, his gazed locked on hers. The red-hot lust consuming her body was mirrored back to her from his penetrating stare. Suddenly she was overcome by something so much more powerful than want. She *wanted* to be successful in her career. She *wanted* to make her daddy proud. Before this, she thought she *wanted* Trace to look at her like he was right now. But she was past those feelings now. This was a deep aching to the point of painful, physical *need*.

She maintained eye contact as she dropped her panties into the washing machine. "Forget something?" she asked softly. Trace reached past her, still not looking away from her face, though she could feel how badly he wanted to, and tossed the briefs he'd been holding into the machine.

"I thought you'd already be in the shower." His steely glare hardened but Kylie didn't miss the tremor in his voice.

"Sorry to disappoint you," she quipped, breaking eye contact to pick her towel up off the floor. Suddenly she was very aware that her skin wasn't one connected entity like she'd always believed. It was made of a zillion tiny individual cells that singed and tingled violently as Trace scrutinized them.

"Nothing about you is disappointing," he rasped. An inferno raged between her thighs and she just barely resisted the urge to grab the towel around his waist and pull him to her.

"Two compliments in one day. If I didn't know better, I'd think you were starting to like me," she said as she wrapped the thick white terrycloth around herself. Now that she was covered, his eyes raked over every inch of her body, touching all the places she wanted his hands to. He'd caught a glimpse and it seemed he'd liked what he saw, whether he wanted to admit it or not.

"Please go get in the shower now," his strained voice pleaded.

Rejection spread like lava over her exposed flesh. Until she looked down at the front of his towel. "Seriously, go. I need a minute."

"Just one minute?" she asked, stepping closer to him. "Well, that is disappointing."

Trace closed his eyes as Kylie ran a finger lightly over his bare chest, but he didn't move or even flinch. Drunk with power, she took another step closer. His skin was hot like she'd anticipated, and pulled taut over his muscles. She desperately wanted to replace her finger with her tongue.

"Shower with me?" she suggested softly, careful to keep any hint of pleading out of her voice. Not that she wasn't prepared to beg if need be. An intense throbbing had taken over her entire body. It was like nothing she'd ever felt before and it had her seconds away from crying out for him to touch her.

But he shook his head no, eyes still closed, the muscles in his jaw clenching almost in time with her own pulsating ache.

"Please look at me," she whispered. He opened his eyes. They burned so fiercely she feared she might melt under the heat. Her body warmed to a dangerously high temperature from the inside out. If she wasn't so turned on, she'd be scared.

This would make her like all the others and she knew it, but she wanted him because of who he really was. The guy she'd seen here at his home and through his sisters' eyes. Not because of the fame or the reputation. More like in spite of them. In her mind, that made their circumstances different. And it wasn't like she was trying to marry him or anything. After tomorrow night, who knew if she'd ever even see him again? She sure as hell didn't, and that made her want him that much more.

"Then just make love to me and I'll shower after, all by myself." Her words were still lingering in the air when Trace let loose a guttural growl and lifted her off the floor. She wrapped her legs around him as if it were natural instinct and gave in to the urge to claim his mouth as hers. Because she had to.

His thick wet tongue pressed hot into her mouth and she heard herself moan. She hadn't known a kiss could feel like love but Trace made a job of it, licking and sucking and gently biting at her lips until he'd tasted every inch of her.

He pressed her against the wall in the hallway outside of the laundry room and trailed firm kisses from her jaw to her throat. She moaned again loudly, wondering if normal people moaned during kissing. She massaged her way up the hard arms that held her until she reached his neck. Running her fingers through his thick hair, she relished in its softness. He groaned and she covered his mouth again.

He smelled of damp earth and tasted of water and want. It was beyond a bad idea and Kylie knew that anything that felt this amazingly good would be followed immediately by hell to pay. But, God forgive her, it was worth it. When they finally made it to the shower, she was trembling with need.

Trace turned the water on ten degrees past scalding and Kylie braced herself as the water covered her. Pulling her close from behind, he devoured her neck with his mouth and a whimper tore from deep inside of her. Her knees threatened to give out but arms of steel steadied her as he turned her around to face him.

"You're even more beautiful soaking wet." His voice was so thick and deep it almost sent her careening over the edge then and there.

"Please, Trace. I need you. *Now*," she begged shamelessly.

As if he'd waited a lifetime for those exact words, he grabbed her and lifted her again, pressing her against the tile shower wall. It was cold against her back but she was burning up.

"Aw hell," Trace groaned, along with a few other choice words.

"What? What's wrong?" Kylie was entering full-blown panic mode trying to figure out what she'd done wrong.

"Condom." Trace looked around as if one would appear in the shower.

"Um, are there any under the sink?"

"No, Kylie. There aren't. I don't bring women here." He lowered her to standing and braced an arm on the wall beside her head.

Oh. And *oh*, that made her want this so much more. She didn't even think she *could* want this more, but there it was. "Trace, I'm on the pill. Have been for the past year."

"What are you saying?"

“I think you know,” she said softly, tensing for the awkward dose of rejection about to spill out all over her. The water pouring over his perfect skin made Kylie want to lick every inch of him.

“Kylie, listen to me. I do not fuck without condoms. Ever.”

“So don’t fuck me, Trace. Make love to me.”

The man who had eleven number one hits in the first few years of his career, who’d escorted models, actresses, and countless beautiful women to red carpet award shows and other celebrity-filled events, who appeared perfectly comfortable in the middle of what Kylie considered an orgy, looked completely and utterly lost.

“I-I don’t make love either, Kylie Lou.”

“You could try,” she said softly. “Please? For me?” There it was. The undeniable proof that she’d fallen. Far and hard. She was begging. And she never, ever begged. For anything. Ever.

“I don’t know if I can.” Trace let his eyes drink in every inch of her wet naked body.

She ran a hand slowly down his chiseled arm. Softly at first, before gripping him harder and pressing herself closer to him. “I’ll be gentle with you.”

Trace’s answering moan echoed off the walls. “This how it’s going to be with you? You making me do all the things I’ve managed to avoid my whole life?”

Kylie smiled the most seductive grin she could manage. “Hope so.” Placing her mouth on his, she pulled him back to where they were before. Back to her wet writhing body, that ached with a need only he could soothe.

Trace used one hand to clutch her chin and hold her still while he explored her mouth with his tongue and his other to open the slick, folded flesh between her thighs.

Kylie’s whimpers grew louder than the water raining down on them. She spread her legs further, giving him full access. He moaned into her mouth as he slid a finger into her opening.

“Maybe I changed my mind,” Kylie said against his lips. Trace pulled back but she didn’t let him go far. “Maybe I want you to fuck me instead.”

“All in due time, darlin’.” As soon as the words were out of his mouth he dropped to his knees and used his fingers to open her even further. Glancing down at him kneeling before her in the steamed up shower almost caused her to come right then. His thick wet tongue pushed against her in slow, torturous licks.

"*Oh my God.*" Suddenly she was frantic and panting. "Yes, I definitely changed my mind." Trace licked her harder, dipping his tongue inside of her.

She was definitely not going to live through this. Kylie's legs threatened to give out and she reached for something to grab. A bar on the shower door was helpful but probably wouldn't last long under her death grip.

Reaching up to cup her breasts, Trace licked his way north until he was standing. "My sweet, wet girl. So tough on the outside and so soft and sweet on the inside." He clamped his mouth down on hers and Kylie tasted herself on his lips. Metal clanged and the sound echoed around them. Yep, the bar on the shower door was now hanging from only one end.

Trace either didn't notice or didn't care. He lifted her above him, smiling when she wrapped her legs around his waist. Her stomach muscles clenched tightly in anticipation. Fear washed over her. *What if she was bad at it?*

Kylie felt the tip of him entering her and she bit down on his bottom lip. She needed him inside of her *now*. Her inner walls were pulling and gripping him tightly as he pressed inward. God, he was huge and thick. She couldn't imagine how the whole thing would actually fit since his *finger* had felt like a stretch.

Trace groaned, letting the sound out slowly as he pushed inside of her in one deliciously painful thrust. Something pinched and tore and the intense pressure was too damn much to handle quietly. Whimpers of mingled pain and pleasure escaped Kylie's throat. She clenched her eyes shut in an attempt to survive it. When she let herself look into his, they were wide with panic.

"Kylie? What the hell? *Oh God.*" He shook his head and Kylie clenched him tighter. She should've told him. But then he might have turned her down. He slammed his hand hard against the shower wall, causing her to flinch.

She couldn't stand the sadness she saw filling his eyes as he shook his head back and forth. Like he hated himself. Her mouth opened and she said everything and anything she could think of to make it better, so he wouldn't stop. "I wanted this, wanted you. Wanted you so bad, Trace. I needed it to be you. *Please.*"

The veins in his neck bulged as he closed his eyes and inhaled sharply. "Dammit, Kylie. Stop," he commanded without looking at her.

She tried, but she couldn't force her body to quit sliding up and down his length in a desperate effort to get him to the place she needed. When she did it was pure molten pleasure. It felt so good Kylie lost the power of speech for a moment. And then she was hit with an overwhelming wave of panic. Because it was too damn good. The kind of good that ruins you for everyone and everything else. Nothing would ever be this good again. When he finally opened his eyes, the look he gave her told her that was exactly what he'd intended. Until he'd realized she was a virgin. Trace grabbed her arms, forcing her to stop moving. The cold sting of rejection seized her.

Please no.

Once she was still, he withdrew from inside of her and lowered her to standing. Kylie had to bite the inside of her cheek to keep from crying when he turned and shut the water off.

Before she could figure out how to convince him to finish what they'd started, he opened the shower door. The cold blast of air hit her so hard she lost her breath. Wrapping her arms around her wet naked body in an attempt to stop the shivering that was rocking her, she watched helplessly as he stepped out of the shower.

"Cold?" he asked softly.

Talking equaled tears coming, so she nodded and looked away. A surprised squeal escaped her throat when she felt herself being lifted again. Strong sure arms carried her bride-over-the-threshold style to the king-sized bed in the next room.

He laid her on the mattress and stared down at her naked form. "You're too damn beautiful for your own good. Hell, you're too damn beautiful for *my* own good."

Kylie smiled nervously up at him, unsure of what was coming. "My hair's going to get your pillows all wet," she said, leaning up so he could put a towel under her if he wanted.

"Baby, when we're done, I hope you've soaked the whole damn mattress."

Relief flooded her entire body. As did a much needed warmth. Before she had time to laugh at him for being so crazy, Trace straddled her, cutting off anything else she'd planned to say. The thick ridge of his erection pressed against her. "It's your first time, Kylie. We're going to do this right." Leaning down, he sucked each of her breasts into his mouth, pulling each nipple with his teeth until she moaned his name.

Heat began to build between her legs as he slid off of her. She was warm and wet and ready. Spreading her knees apart with his hand, Trace eyed the juncture at her thighs like a forbidden dessert. "Even this is beautiful," he said reverently, trailing a finger through her wetness.

Kylie blushed and twitched at the unusual compliment. "Trace." Her knees tried to snap together but he held her open.

"It is. It's perfect." Lowering his mouth to her, he placed gentle licks between her legs until she was arching off the bed. His tongue seemed to be apologizing for the rough treatment his dick had just given her. Not that she was complaining about either. Though his mouth on her oversensitive flesh was so intense, her body strained to pull away.

"Where are you trying to go, darlin'?"

"Mmm." She couldn't answer because she couldn't form any actual words at the moment. She wanted to touch him but her hands were fisted in the comforter beneath her. If she let go, she feared she'd rocket out into space. She was losing control. Part of her hated the feeling. But that part could shut the hell up because what Trace was doing to her was so good she was seconds away from screaming.

Sliding his hands upwards, he tickled her inner thighs and she squirmed. Still licking her clit gently, he pressed a finger deep inside and Kylie's body stiffened. Moans and whimpers and sounds she couldn't recreate if her life depended on it, tore from her throat. Pleasure ripped down the middle of her so hard she gave into the urge to scream just to release some of the pressure. Trace didn't even flinch as she rocked and jerked, nearly kneeing him in the head in an attempt to get some relief from the unrelenting assault of his mouth.

"Oh no, baby. We're not even close to being done," he growled against her center.

Oh God.

She'd have to beg him then. Her words came out in a frantic rush. "Trace, *oh God*. Please. Trace, I can't take anymore. Please. *Please*."

But he didn't stop. He added another finger inside her and increased the pressure of his tongue. It was too much. Her thoughts fled and she lost herself in a sea of swirling ecstasy. The room was spinning hard and fast, or maybe just the bed was, but she couldn't figure out how to make it stop. His mouth moved upward and he replaced his tongue with his thumb on her clit. He braced his muscular frame above her smaller one as his thumb moved in tantalizing circles. His breath tickled her face. "Look at me, Kylie Lou. I want to look into those beautiful blues when you come."

She forced her eyes open and met his sweltering stare. Her mouth tried to form a word, a plea, something. But nothing came. Actually, *she* came. But no words did. Trace locked her in his gaze as her body trembled and convulsed of its own accord. He pulled his fingers out of her slowly and she whimpered at the absence.

"Can you handle more, baby?" he asked just before he sucked his fingers into his mouth. The same fingers that were covered in her wetness. *Jesus.* His eyes held a challenge she hoped she could meet. But she was too weak to answer out loud so she just nodded. *Yes, please.*

This time when he slid himself inside of her, it didn't hurt at all. Her hips rose, rocking in the same slow, rhythmic pace he set for them. Finally able to release the handfuls of comforter, she wrapped her arms around him, digging her fingers into his back in an effort to pull him down on her.

"No, no, no, little miss I call the shots. You've been demanding and in control for long enough. My turn now." Reaching behind him, he pulled her hands away and gripped her wrists firmly enough to cause a slight pinch of pain. He pinned them above her head and continued sinking into her and withdrawing while staring into her eyes from above.

Leaning down, he whispered into her ear. "When I'm finished, you'll barely be able to stand me *not* being inside of you."

chapter TWENTY THREE

EVERYTHING would be different between them now and for that reason, Kylie never wanted to leave his arms, his bed, or his house. Maybe for a few other reasons, too. For the first time in a long time, she felt protected, safe. *Home.* She was also feeling pretty pissed off at herself. She should not be letting herself want this. Sleeping with him was one thing, wanting more than that was just outright asinine.

"Everything okay?" he murmured into her hair as he held her naked body against his.

She snuggled down into the covers, wiggling her backside against his crotch. Who knew spooning could be so hot?

"Again?" he asked, not bothering to keep the shock out of his voice. This would be the third time. Trace's mouth met her bare shoulder with a hot wet kiss.

Kylie purred softly. "Mmm, maybe, if you're up for it, old man. But we should probably get going soon." *Back to reality*, she thought bitterly.

"Ah to be young and free," his warm voice teased as he kissed her neck. Oh God. Free. Could she ever really be free of Darla? Since their discussion earlier, nagging thoughts about what Darla might try to do if Kylie garnered any type of success had been plaguing her. Now was so not the time, but he deserved to know the truth.

"Listen, Trace, about that—"

"Hold that thought." He grabbed his vibrating phone off the nightstand.

She didn't even remember him getting it. He must've gotten it at some point when she'd dozed off.

"Hi, Pauly. Yeah, working on that now. Okay, okay, relax. We'll be there soon." He paused and ran his hand down the length of Kylie's side. "Yeah I know," he snapped into the phone, the sharpness of his voice contrasting with the gentleness of his touch. She heard a click before Pauly had finished talking.

She twisted around so she could look at him. "Did you just hang up on him?"

"I did."

"Trace!"

"Well, he was ruining the moment. Where were we?"

Kylie opened her mouth to finish her sentence from earlier but looking into his eyes stopped her cold. They were the same stormy color they'd been that night at The Rum Room. This might be all she ever got. Talking could wait.

"We were right about here," she told him, pressing herself against him once more. He was right. She already couldn't stand for him not to be inside of her. This would probably be the last time, she thought to herself, so she wanted it to be everything.

"PAULY has called me eleven times," Kylie told Trace as they wolfed down their burgers on the drive back to the bus.

"He's just stressed we won't make it in time to rehearse at Tin Roof. He'll calm down once we get there." His confidence was mildly reassuring, but Kylie didn't mention the texts Pauly was sending in rapid-fire succession telling her to get as far as possible from Trace and call him ASAP.

When they pulled into the RV lot where the tour bus was parked, Trace shut off the engine but didn't make a move to get out.

When our feet hit the ground this will all be just a memory and nothing more. They'd do their last show and go their separate ways. Something deep inside of her ached in the way it had when the police had told her about her dad. *My soul*, she realized. Letting go of Trace after having him for even less than twenty-four hours was hurting her soul. *Because I am obviously outside my ever-loving mind.*

Trace didn't seem to be in a hurry to exit the truck either. Even though it was beginning to feel as if there wasn't enough oxygen in the cab for both of them. "Kylie? You okay?"

She couldn't risk crying, not now, after everything. So she just shook her head. *No.*

"Is it Pauly? 'Cause I promise, he'll be fine once this last show ends and wraps this tour up smoothly."

Smoothly. *Huh.* The thought of it ending now felt jagged and razor sharp to her. "I know. I'm sure you're right," she said quietly.

He stopped wadding the paper wrapper from his sandwich and stared at her for a moment. "Then why do you look terrified of getting out of this truck?"

Kylie took a deep breath. There was already one lie between them. She couldn't stand to add another. "Music has been my…everything, for as long as I can remember. It's the only connection I have left to my dad." She paused to swallow the lump ascending into her esophagus. "There have been times when I've chosen it over food and shelter. I'd take it over air if I could survive." It was the truth. She'd live, breathe, and eat it if she could.

"Kylie, it's fine. I prom—"

"That's not it," she said, shaking her head and staring straight out of the windshield to avoid the intensity of his probing eyes. "I'm not afraid of losing music—no one can really take that from me, not even Pauly."

"Then what—"

"It's always come first, been what's made every painful thing bearable. Before today, there was never anything I'd have even thought about doing for a second if it meant risking my shot." She paused, as startled by her own realization as he was probably about to be. "But if I could relive the past twenty-four hours over again every day for the rest of my life...I'd give it up altogether."

I'm afraid of losing you, she wanted to add but didn't because it would make her seem pathetic. And also because Pauly had stormed off of the bus and was heading straight for them. He didn't look angry like she expected him to. He looked…panicked.

Trace got out of the truck without saying a word. She flinched when the door slammed shut. She watched as he made his way to her door, trying to soothe Pauly the whole way. It didn't appear to be working.

"Don't touch her!" Pauly shouted at Trace when he opened her door and reached in to help her out of the cab.

Trace jerked his head towards his manager. "Jesus, Pauly, what the hell is wrong with you?"

"You," Pauly seethed in her direction, "have a visitor."

chapter TWENTY FOUR

"WELL, as I live and breathe," Darla drawled as soon as Kylie stepped onto the bus. "Mr. Corbin, I'm a big fan of yours. It's truly a pleasure to meet you. Everyone back in Pride can hardly believe our little Kylie here is touring with such a big star."

"Um, thanks." Trace shook the woman's hand, shooting Kylie a puzzled look. *God take me now, please.*

"What the hell are you doing here?" Kylie blurted out. She and Darla had never really been anything more than barely civil to each other, and after the last time she'd seen the woman, she didn't see the point of even bothering with that.

"Well now, Kylie, I think the better question is what exactly are *you* doing here? And according to the interviewer from *Country Weekly*, I should be asking exactly what, or rather who, you've been doing while you've been here."

Her stepmother had on a tight red tank top and Kylie's mother's pearls. Took the phrase 'seeing red' to a whole new level.

"Since you and I are nothing, I can't see how anything I do is really any of your business." Kylie knew she was snarling and that wasn't exactly the version of herself she wanted Trace or Pauly to see, but it really couldn't be helped.

"Oh darlin,' I'm not here for you," Darla informed her, using her best southern belle patronizing tone. "I'm here to protect poor Mr. Corbin here from a sneaky little snake in cowgirl boots before she bites him the same way she did my poor Leo and Jakeykins."

"What's going on, Kylie?" Trace asked, his head turning from her to Darla to Pauly and back around again.

The mention of Leo made Kylie flinch. He was the worst one. The reason she had to put a bolt lock on her bedroom door.

Clearly tired of the charade, Pauly blurted out, "Mrs. Ryans here has some information about Kylie that she is willing to keep quiet for the right amount of money."

All the blood rushed to Kylie's head as if Darla were hanging her upside down.

"What kind of information?" Trace asked, directing his attention to Pauly.

"She hasn't shared all the details with me yet," the weary looking manager answered.

"How much do you want, Darla? Because right now I'm basically working for the price of what it costs me to travel and perform. I haven't received any money yet but I will give you whatever you want as soon as I can, provided that you stay the hell out of my life so long as we both shall live." Her heart slammed against her chest, seemingly as desperate to escape the situation as she was. She was wilting quickly under the heat of Trace's glare.

She turned to him with pleading in her eyes. "I tried to tell you before. This is my—"

"Mother," Darla interrupted. "Stepmother of course, as I'm nowhere near old enough to have a child Kylie's age."

It was exactly as dramatic as Darla had intended it to be. Trace's pupils widened and constricted and his chest heaved in and out with each breath.

"It's just you, huh?" Trace said, snorting in disbelief, or maybe disgust. Kylie wasn't sure.

"Kylie told us she didn't have any living relatives," Pauly said, eyeing Darla as if he thought she might be lying.

"Mr. Corbin, I hate to be the one to tell you, but Kylie here is quite the liar. This isn't the first time she's lied and seduced older men to get what she wanted. I'm sure it won't be the last."

Trace just shook his head as if that would clear out the confusion. "Seduced?" he mumbled more to himself than anyone else.

How could anyone know yet? It had just freaking happened and Kylie hadn't even processed it herself.

Filled with five years' worth of anguish, Kylie lunged at the woman she hated with everything she had.

"You are a crazy bitch, you ruined my dad's life, and you will not come here and ruin mine!" Kylie roared, reaching for her mother's pearls. She felt hair and flesh barely in her grasp before Pauly yanked her back.

"Lawsuit, Kylie. You have to *think*," he said sternly into her ear.

"I hate you! I wish my dad never met you! I wish it had been you instead of him!" She screeched at Darla from the security of Pauly's, and now Trace's, grasp.

"Well, I think that proves my point, gentlemen," Darla said, righting her hair and fingering Kylie's mother's necklace. "And frankly, I don't see any reason I should lie for a disrespectful brat who is clearly not mature enough to be managing a career of her own."

An animalistic sound ripped from Kylie's core as she lunged again.

"Get her out of here, Pauly. Fuck!" Trace yelled as his hands tightened around her arms. "Take her in my room."

Pauly spoke soothing words into Kylie's ear as he all but dragged her back to Trace's room. She could hear Trace asking Darla for a specific dollar amount to keep quiet about whatever she supposedly knew about Kylie. "Enough to fill a best-seller," Kylie heard the woman say. Something about a Non-Disclosure Agreement was being mentioned just as Pauly closed Trace's door behind them.

Kylie pressed against it to listen. Tears of rage burned trails of shame down her face. She didn't even bother wiping them. "This is extortion, isn't it? Can she really do this to me?"

"This is why we asked if you had any family members or things in your past that we should know about. It's not uncommon for relatives to pop out of the woodwork when someone gets a little notice. But what she said about seducing older men, is there anything to that? Please tell me this wasn't some type of plan to make Trace look bad." He didn't even look at her as he made the accusation.

Kylie slid down the length of the door until her bottom reached the carpet. "Is that really what you think of me, Pauly? Seriously?"

"I don't know what to think, Kylie. It's just a messed up situation and I have to do what's best for Trace." He rubbed his temples for a moment and looked up at her with bloodshot eyes. "Lots of larger labels have been known to take the low road when they want to get rid of someone. Even so low as to plant a girl to sing his song at an open mic night to get his attention, only for her to later release a sex tape of them. This is country music. Something like that would ruin him."

"Jesus Christ." Kylie shook her head to keep the ugliness of his words out. "She kicked me out and I lost my job in the same day. I had nothing, no one, and nowhere to go. I used what little money I had to get a hotel room and a waitressing job when I got to Nashville. My plan was to save up to record a demo and go from there. There was no way I could've known Trace would be there that night. Hell, Clive didn't even know." She squeezed her eyes shut, thinking about the impossibility of her fate.

"What was I supposed to do, Pauly, when you dangled the answer to my prayers, my freaking life's dream, in front of me? Tell you I had a crazy bitch of a stepmother, lose my dream, and go back to having nothing? What would you have done?"

"Swear to me she doesn't have anything on you that could hurt Trace," he said quietly.

"I swear. A few of the random men she constantly had coming in and out of her bedroom paid a little too much attention to me and she was jealous. She's a horrible woman. My dad's grave was barely covered when she started dating again. All she wants is money and I will pay her whatever it takes to keep her out of my life."

"People like this," Pauly began and then stopped and shook his head. He ran a hand through his thinning hair. "I can't manage you. Not now. It's a conflict of interest, but I know someone who can. And you're going to need a lawyer in case she ever tries this again."

Kylie nodded, finally wiping her tears. "Just tell me what to do."

"Right, 'cause you listen so well." He aimed a pointed glare at the blue shirt of Trace's she was still wearing.

Yeah, okay. Truth hurts. "I will this time. I'll do whatever you say."

"If you really mean that, I will have Chaz Michaelson meet us in South Carolina. He's a manager that has already expressed some interest in you and he's good, has some major connections in Nashville. He's young but solid, trustworthy. But I need you to do something for me."

"Anything," she promised, swiping a hand under her nose and standing.

"Keep quiet about whatever happened between you and Trace in Georgia."

"Done."

"And stay away from Trace until this tour is completely over and whatever your stepmother has put out to the media dies down."

Anything except that, she thought. Like Trace would want anything to do with her now that he'd just seen Darla bring out her inner trailer park.

She nodded. "I care about him, Pauly. I wouldn't do anything to hurt him."

The manager just rolled his neck and looked at her for a long minute. "It's usually the people we care about that we hurt the most."

KYLIE didn't have time to respond to Pauly's comment. Trace burst through the door, barely wasting a second to glance at her and then spoke to his manager as if she wasn't there.

"She wanted fifty grand," he said with an eye roll. "Like that was ever going to happen. I told her Kylie was just another one hit wonder and she would be lucky if anyone even remembered her name after this tour ended, much less made any real money. She settled for half that and signed the NDA. I told her I'd have someone send her a copy in case she got any ideas about writing any tell-alls in the future."

Kylie didn't recognize this man. The one talking to Pauly like she was nothing. He knew the business, though, and if this was what he thought about her career, then he was probably right. *It's recently come to my attention that you've actually got some talent,* he'd said to her outside his mini studio. But that was before he'd screwed her.

No, it was more than that. She knew in her heart he hadn't been planning on that. But he'd been more than clear about one thing. Darla or no Darla, he didn't do relationships. What had happened was a one and done and she was going to have to deal with it like a big girl. Pauly nodded like he agreed with Trace's assessment but Kylie spoke before he could voice his opinion out loud.

She lifted her chin and aimed her words at the middle of the room. "I'll pay you back as soon as I can, if anyone remembers my name after tomorrow, that is."

Kylie heard Trace say something but she couldn't make it out and didn't know if she even wanted to. She slipped out of his room and into hers, locking the latch behind her. It wasn't necessary. No one came to check on her.

THE sound of pounding on her door woke Kylie before dawn. *Please let it be him*. She didn't even care if he wanted to yell and cuss. She just wanted to hash it all out so she would know where she stood.

"Kylie, come on. You have a Skype date," Pauly's voice announced.

The Skype date was with Cora and she was in full make-up running all through modes of damage control as Kylie struggled to focus on her image through blurry eyes. Basically Cora just wanted to know if anything Darla was saying was true and if the woman was going to be showing up causing problems.

"Cora, I swear, she is a lying bitch of the lowest form. I never seduced any of her "men" or anything even remotely like that. And I have no ties to her in any way now."

"Tell me the truth, kid, because the shit will hit the fan sooner or later and I could do a lot better by you and Trace both if I know what's coming. Are you sleeping together?"

An involuntary flinch rocked her slightly and Cora nodded. "Okay, well, how about you knock it off until all this dies down? Your wicked step-monster made some seriously damaging comments to a few reporters and Trace really doesn't need that right now. And frankly, neither do you."

Kylie nodded and hoped Cora could tell through the pixelated image. "Pretty sure it was a one-time thing," she said quietly, not sure if the MacBook's mic even picked it up.

"Relax, you're not the first girl to fall for walking sin in tight jeans."

It was the first kind thing anyone had said to her since Darla's little visit. Kylie wondered if Cora was referring to her own experience with Trace specifically. Not that it was any of her business.

"Thanks," she said quietly.

"Okay, well, go back to bed. You look like hell. It's one more show, Kylie. You'll be fine. We'll talk more later about what's next. An all-girl Random Road Trip tour sponsored by Vitamin Water has an open spot and I'm going to throw your name in the hat. That okay with you?"

"Um, yeah. Sure," she answered even though it was really too early to even process what Cora was saying.

"And I know Pauly has called Chaz Michaelson out to see you perform in South Carolina. He's great, and you'll love him, but um…maybe don't love him too much 'cause he's gay." With that Cora flashed her perfect smile and disconnected.

When Kylie stood up to head back to her room she thought she saw a shadow in the doorway. Pauly probably.

She went back to bed and lay awake. The only thing connecting her to whoever Trace had been when they were in Georgia was a slight soreness that she hoped would never go away. Because when it did, it would be like it never happened. The one day of happiness she'd had since her dad died, and it was starting to feel like she'd dreamed the whole thing.

Cora knew what had happened and since Pauly had called her, he must know too. She wondered what Trace had told him. Oh well. Not like she was expecting to have much privacy in this business anyways. If random strangers could comment publically about her bra size, no reason her sex life shouldn't be common knowledge. Just made it that much easier to let go. If it had remained a shared secret between her and Trace, she might've been stupid enough to think it actually meant something.

WHEN Kylie woke up from a convoluted dream in which Darla was suing her in court over something that made absolutely no sense, she felt like she hadn't slept in days. Her head throbbed, her eyelids were heavy, and her entire body was stiff.

She stretched and headed to the shower. Once she exited her tiny corner of the world, she realized the bus felt strangely empty. Even Carl, the driver who she knew had three sons and a daughter with his wife Lorna of sixteen years, was missing.

God, he probably hated her now too. In the beginning when Trace behaved as if she had the plague, and Pauly had spent all his time on his phone, Carl had been her only company. Jesus, she was even going to miss him. The list kept growing. Her dad, Lulu, Tonya, even Clive a little, Trace more than she had the strength to admit, Claire Ann, Rae, Pauly, and now Carl. She had to stop talking to people. Period.

And that's when it hit her. As the steamy water rushed over her, she realized all she had to do was close herself off. Just stop volunteering information and contributing to conversations altogether. Trace had acted like that from the beginning and if she'd just been equally as cold right back, none of this ever would've happened.

But giving up the memory of that amazing trip to Macon would be damn near impossible. The party, Rae's excitement just because Kylie was there, the dancing, the writing that was almost as intimate as the sex, the mud fight, and so help her, the love making that was so good she'd worried she was becoming a nymphomaniac.

But it wasn't just that, it was all of it—the whole package. It was a life with someone she loved and a family who accepted and welcomed her in. People who understood how she felt about music and what it meant and what she'd do for it. But they didn't really. She'd seen the disbelief on his face at Darla's words. Trace would never understand why she'd lied about actually having a family member, even if it was a psycho non-blood-related one. Of course not, because in his scenario, he'd been the one who was disowned.

Once again the weight of what she was losing pressed down on her like it had at breakfast that morning in Georgia. It would be so easy to slink down onto the shower floor and just cry. She knew if she let go and gave in she'd never be able to stop. It wasn't like things were going to change.

Not for you, Kylie. Nobody wants you for more than one night.

If the boys she'd fooled around with in pickups and behind the bleachers in high school hadn't wanted people to know they were together, what in God's name had made her think someone like Trace Corbin would be interested? Well, whatever it was, she was done being the naïve hick from Oklahoma. She'd made a promise to her daddy, one she intended to keep.

After her shower there was a black garment bag on her bed. Someone had been in her room.

No more choices apparently.

A champagne-colored dress covered in sequins gleamed from inside. It was actually her size for once but it was cut low in the front and the hem would barely cover her thighs. Fine, she could do this. Be sexy and strong and sing her ass off. Her dad had taught her to work hard at whatever her job was. *I don't care if you're a famous movie star or you clean toilets for a living, Kylie. All that matters is that you give whatever you do everything you have. Never let anyone else out-work you.*

Her dad never would have done what the factory spokesperson had said. Unless he was preoccupied because she was mad at him. Stressed about the fact that she and Darla were always at each other's throats and he was constantly caught in the middle. *Not your fault, Kylie,* a small voice inside her head whispered. But she'd always wondered.

Seventeen years at his job and not a single safety violation. Then one day he forgets to tie a cord securing a steel coil that weighed nearly a ton and he's gone forever.

Well, she wasn't about to shame his memory by throwing away her shot at her dream over a guy, no matter who he was or how she felt about him.

She knew it was a risky thing to do, not to mention unprofessional, but she skipped sound check. She wanted to do a cover of a Kelly Clarkson song that had been stuck in her head and she needed to work on it alone. And she couldn't face him just yet.

She was supposed to go on at seven and the bus was blissfully empty until nearly six. She kept expecting someone to come bitch at her about missing sound check, but no one ever did. It was both a relief and a slap to her ego.

She did her own hair and make-up and slipped on the dress. She looked at the sky high nude stilettos she was supposed to wear and almost laughed out loud. Sure, a fall on her ass should make for great publicity. No thank you. She slipped on her dark brown worn-in cowgirl boots. She was going to do things her way, and if it didn't work out then she'd have no one to blame but herself. No "fight the machine" bitterness that Trace held onto. Just a face in the mirror. She pulled her favorite jean jacket over it and gave her wild curls one more toss. For the first time in a long time she felt like herself, and she was okay with whoever that was.

"KYLIE, thank God." Pauly rushed towards her backstage. "Please tell me you've been with Trace and you both just got back from wherever the hell you were. I won't even be mad, I swear."

Oh no.

"I've been on the bus alone, Pauly," Kylie said slowly. "I haven't talked to Trace once since you told me not to. In fact, I haven't even seen him since I left you guys last night." Unless he was the shadow early this morning after her Skype call with Cora.

"Son of a—"

"What's going on?" she asked, terrified of hearing the answer.

"He's gone," Pauly told her. "We've been looking for him all day and he's not answering his cell."

She had just over an hour before she was supposed to go on. Chaz

Michaelson was going to be there and if she wasn't at her best he wouldn't manage her, and Pauly had already washed his hands of her. The rumors about her and Trace alone had people wary of working with her, according to Cora. But what she'd said in the truck was still true, even after everything.

"What happens if he doesn't show?" she asked Pauly. It was the last show on the tour, so maybe it wasn't that big of a deal.

"Then he's done," Pauly answered, sinking into a sofa chair.

"Well yeah, the tour's over. I mean what will—"

"No, Kylie," Pauly interrupted. "I mean he's *done* done. This tour was supposed to be an arena tour, but with all the bad publicity from the public intox charge last year and the fights and the girls, tickets weren't selling so they downgraded him to small venues in hopes of a comeback. This was literally his last shot and after the no-show in Dallas the label warned him that the next time he cost them money they would drop him."

Damn. Trace was right—it was a machine and if you stopped producing it spit you out. It couldn't end this way for him. She'd seen the look of sheer bliss on his face as he strummed his guitar and worked out lyrics to fit with hers.

"Stall, Pauly. I will find him. He will perform. Don't tell anyone anything, okay?" Kylie demanded as she started to leave.

"No," he said, startling her by standing abruptly and grabbing her arm just before she stepped out of reached. "Kylie, if you don't make it back in time for your performance then you'll be done too. Nashville is like high school—people talk, things get out. Not only will Chaz Michaelson tell everyone you're a flake but there'll be bad blood between you and the label. You signed a contract," he reminded her gently.

"So it's my career or his, Pauly. Is that what you're telling me?"

"No. I am simply pointing out that if you get caught up in his mess and don't get back here before you're supposed to be on stage, then you won't have a leg to stand on when it comes to having a career in country music and there won't be much I can do to help you."

"And what about him? If I perform tonight and he never shows, will there be anything you can do to help him? Can't you talk to someone at the label?"

"I've done everything I can for him—and then some. I've begged, pleaded, apologized, and called in every last favor I had. You can't make someone want this life."

"But he does want it. He's just mad at me and taking it out on himself because that's what he does," she pleaded. It was so clear now. This was Trace's MO. Self-destruct so he won't hurt anyone else. Unless his sideshow fling falls for him, then his asinineness hurts her, too.

"Wait. Stop and think for a second. You want this and you're talented. Don't go looking for him. Don't throw your shot away like he keeps doing. Most people don't get so many."

"I have to," she told him as she slid her arm out of his grasp. "Because this time he's throwing it away because of me."

RUNNING out of The Tin Roof, she thanked the Powers That Be that she hadn't dared worn those stupid ass stilettos. She checked every single bar within walking distance. She was nearly out of time. She had thirty minutes until she was supposed to be on stage.

She slipped her phone out of her jacket pocket and dialed the only person she knew who might help her.

"We had an argument. I can't find him, Rae, and if we both aren't ready to go on stage in the next hour, we can kiss our careers goodbye."

"Oh my God! Tell me what I can do!" Trace's younger sister squealed, clearly worried about her brother but sounding like she was also pretty excited that Kylie had called her.

The gears turned in her head. "I'm sorry to put this on you but I need you to call him and just act casual but concerned. Tell him you spoke with me and I sounded strange, like I was going to do something crazy, hurt myself or something. Just say whatever you have to. I need him to get back to the bus, like *now*."

"Okay, awesome! I'll get to test my acting skills! Maybe I can be in one of your videos!" Yep, she was definitely excited.

"Rae, if this works and your brother will allow it, you can be in every video ever as far as I'm concerned. Call me as soon as you talk to him. Please."

Millennia passed as Kylie stood staring at her phone. Screw standing around. If he did show he was probably going to be drunk. She hopped back on the bus, said a quick hello to Carl, who had also been out looking for Trace, and turned on the Keurig. She brewed three cups and pulled out a thermos she'd found in a cabinet. Her phone buzzed on the counter mid-pour and she nearly scorched herself.

"Did you get ahold of him?"

"Yeah, um, he's on his way. He wouldn't tell me where he was but I could hear voices and music in the background, and he was slurring his words a little."

She'd kind of figured that was the case but it still made her sad. "Okay, well, at least he's coming."

"Yeah, um, Kylie," Trace's sister hesitated. "I had to kind of play it up a lot to get him to say he'd go check on you, like I might've made it sound like you are going to kill yourself before you go on stage if he doesn't come profess his undying love or something so…"

Jesus. "Well that's going to be awkward but no worries, Rae. You did what I asked. I'll tell him I said he was committing career suicide and there was a bad connection and you misunderstood."

"You're really quite the expert at this whole lying thing then, aren't you?" Trace's voice said from behind her.

"Gotta go, Rae. Thank you," Kylie said quietly before disconnecting the call and turning to face a man with pure hatred on his face.

"Well, since you're not on the verge of anything drastic, think I'll go finish my drink now," Trace told her. He wasn't full out slurring but he did sound like his tongue might be heavier than normal.

"Carl, a little help please," she called out to the driver. Thankfully, the bus driver had a good forty pounds on Trace. He stood in the doorway successfully blocking the exit.

"You're fired," Trace growled as he glowered at the man Kylie thought of as a big teddy bear.

"He has four kids to support, Trace," she reminded him. "You're not fired, Carl. Hang tight. He'll forget all about this by tomorrow."

"Just hear the girl out, man, for Pete's sakes," Carl grumbled as he ambled out of Trace's way.

His fists were clenched and his jaw was doing that clenchy twitching thing, but Trace stayed where he was, standing in the aisle of the bus.

"Can we sit please?" she asked, gesturing at the semi-circle booth across from her.

Trace strode over to her and sat but his eyes were flat black and empty. *He's this mad because I didn't tell him I had a crazy stepmother?*

"I'm sorry I lied, truly I am, but it was a necessary lie at the time. You met Darla, and you know my situation. I never planned to meet you, to get this amazing opportunity. What was I supposed to do, Trace? Risk missing out on it because of her?"

"What you were supposed to do was tell the goddamned truth and not play some stupid fucking mind games with me and then trick me in to sleeping with you so that you and your stepmother could blackmail me." The sneer on his face was the only expression Kylie had ever seen him wear that made him appear anything even close to unattractive. She took several deep breaths. He'd been drinking. He couldn't possibly mean what he was saying. "And then you use my family to lure me here so you can what? Lie to me some more? What the hell do you want from me, whoever the fuck you are?"

Kylie couldn't sit this close to this awful man anymore. She slid out of the booth and stood. "All I want is for you to forget you ever met me, forget everything that happened, and go out on stage and be Trace Corbin, the brand, like you said. Make the label happy so that you can keep recording and doing what you love instead of ending up angry and alone and bitter like your dad."

She knew that last part was probably a step too far. But it was true.

"What I love." Trace laughed an ugly laugh she hoped she'd never hear again. "You know what I love? Lying whores who think they know everything. You and your stepmom aren't so different. Actually, you're all the damn same."

Kylie's knees buckled and a noise that an animal being tortured might make escaped her throat. Even Carl flinched. She couldn't even open her mouth to ask *who* was all the damn same. When Darla had called her a whore, it had been a lie and she knew it. But Trace had been with plenty of women. If the way she'd behaved during sex with him made her a whore, he would know.

At some point Pauly had stepped onto the bus and was just watching the nightmare unfold.

Tears pinched her eyes and her entire body trembled, but there was no way she was letting alcohol-fueled courage tear her down. "Pardon me, but you can go straight to hell, *Tracey* Corbin. I made a mistake, but you know what? I wouldn't change a damn thing because I risked everything I had which, okay, wasn't a whole hell of a lot, for what I love, for who I love, and for something I've dreamed of since I was a little girl. Now I may not be as perfect as you, but I've learned not to throw away opportunities to say what's in my heart. I did that once and I'll have to live with that forever. So I'm going to tell you, sorry sonofabitch that you are, exactly what I feel."

Kylie took a deep breath and stared down at a large man who suddenly seemed very small. "I don't know this version of you, and frankly, I don't care for him. But I do know Rae and Claire Ann, and I know they deserve a hell of a lot better from you than this. So do Pauly, Cora, the band, and your fans. Maybe I don't, and that's fine, because even though I meant what I said in the truck yesterday and I still mean it, I am done with you after today if you don't go on that stage and sing like your damned life depends on it tonight." Her voice shook audibly but she couldn't have stopped the rest of what she had to say even if she'd wanted to. "Anyone who behaves the way you do, running off to self-destruct in a bottle of whatever the hell you've been drinking, is a selfish coward. And whether or not you think my career is going anywhere, I am going to damn well try. Matter of fact, I will try even harder just to spite you." Kylie struggled to catch her breath. The lack of oxygen had her seeing dark spots behind her eyes.

"Good for you, waitress," he sneered. "I'd high-five you but I'm afraid you might try and sue me for assault."

Kylie couldn't speak because of the lump crushing her vocal cords. She'd said everything there was to say, and damn it to hell, she couldn't reach him. Couldn't get through to the guy who'd brought her breakfast in bed, wiped her tears, and protected the women he loved.

When she did finally find her voice, it came out raspy and laced with hurt. "How dare you think for one second that I would ever do anything to hurt you? My whole life, I've never intentionally hurt another person. You think what you do is okay? Like it doesn't hurt people who care about you to see you destroy everything good in your life? You're wrong." She stared at him, hoping to see a glimpse of the man she knew was somewhere in there. "Who are you?" she whispered.

"Guess you don't know me as well as you thought, huh?"

"No, and you know what? I don't even want to anymore." For a moment they just stared at each other. Then Kylie realized she'd just lied. She did want to know him. Even this horrible version of him. So she could help him find a way to stop doing this to himself.

"That was a lie, what I just said," she admitted quietly. "But I wish it were true."

Trace's eye's widened noticeably, but he didn't move. "Just add it to the list of all the other lies you've told. Hell, what's one more?"

"Here," she said, grabbing the thermos of coffee she'd brewed from the counter and slamming it down on the table in front of him. "Sober up, or don't. I'm done."

She glanced towards the front of the bus. Carl looked like he might be about to cry and Pauly was just struck dumb and staring blankly. She knew she should get the hell off this bus but there was something else. Something she had to say to that other man, the one she was right in the middle of falling in love with when everything went to hell in a heartbeat.

Swallowing every ounce of pride she had, she slid into the booth next to Trace. He leaned back and glared at her as if she were diseased. He might as well have plunged a fist into her chest and squeezed her heart with all his might.

"What I didn't get to say yesterday in the truck," she began in a whisper, "was that I didn't want to get out because I was terrified of losing you. Not that I had you really, but as much as I love music, and believe me, I love it deep down into my soul, I loved being with you more." She felt the hot tears escape and roll down her cheeks, but it didn't matter anymore. He'd already seen everything else she had.

"Next Monday I will turn nineteen. For the first time ever, my dad won't be there to sing to me and I won't be able to stop wondering if I had done things differently, told you about Darla up front, if we'd be celebrating my birthday together. Or if I am just the kind of girl that nobody will ever want more than once."

Bone crushing pain sucked the air from her lungs but she continued. "And a day won't pass from here until who knows when that I won't wish that if that were true, I could relive that one day in Macon with you over and over again. Maybe even more than I wish for my daddy back or to make the best country music album that I possibly can to honor his memory. He just wanted me to be happy, and for the first time since he died, I was."

Kylie wiped her tears and breathed a small sigh of relief. Trace still leaned away from her, but he was in there. The man she could love. Maybe already did love. Or something close to it. She'd seen a lightning flash of him somewhere near the end of her speech.

"You're young. You'll get over it," he said softly, not looking at her at all anymore.

She scooted out of the booth once more and forced a small smile. "I hope you get your shit together. I really do."

"Kylie," Pauly called from the other end of the bus. "It's time to go."

"Goodbye, Trace," she whispered. But he didn't say it back. He was just a statue staring at his hands on the table in front of him. Kylie took a deep breath. It was okay. She was okay. At least it wouldn't be her who left things unsaid this time.

No words caught in her throat as she prepared to perform. Her voice wouldn't fail like in her nightmares and she didn't even have an ounce of nervousness left in her. She wiped her face with the tissue Pauly had handed her on the way out and checked her body for cuts and bruises. How there wasn't any physical evidence of the bloody battle she'd just endured with Trace Corbin she didn't know, because she stepped on stage feeling like she'd been sliced clean open and emptied of everything inside of her.

KYLIE'S cover of Kelly Clarkson's *Dark Side* was by far the hardest song she'd ever performed. It had been in her head for a while now, and she'd worked out the acoustic arrangement perfectly. But Trace's face, both of them actually, warm, open, and tender, next to cold, closed and angry, wouldn't leave her. *It's hard to know what can become if you give up* almost sent her running off stage. When she finished, roaring applause nearly deafened her.

"Whew, thank y'all. That was a tough one. I just had my heart broken, and damn, that Kelly knows how to pour salt in the wound." Several people threw her an audible pity party. "Nah, it's cool. I'm going to Taylor Swift his ass in the next song I write. So don't y'all worry about me." The audience whistled and a single face came in to view from the back of the dark room. He was there, watching her perform. She just didn't know which version of him was listening.

After she finished her set, Chaz Michaelson was waiting for her. He was as amazing as Pauly and Cora had both promised. Five minutes into their conversation he had Kylie scheduled to meet with the Vitamin Water people to see if she would be a good fit for The Random Road Trip tour.

She'd have to maintain a blog and ride a bus with a bunch of chicks, but after what she'd been through with Trace the past few weeks, it sounded perfect. Plus it would be a way to earn some money to pay for a place to live and studio time for recording her demo. She'd leave in three weeks and visit twenty-three states and thirty-five cities. If she did well on the tour, maybe she'd get the attention of an agent and a label that might be interested in signing her. It would be an insane schedule but Kylie needed to stay busy or she feared she'd drown in heartbreak.

During her lonely bus time she'd finished the song she and Trace had worked on together. *The Other Side of Me* was their song even more now than it had been when they'd started, but she knew she had to let it go or she'd try to use it as a way to see him again in a moment of weakness. Recording with him was not something she ever planned to be strong enough for.

FOR TRACE AND PAULY, she wrote on the outside of the envelope. Inside were the completed lyrics and a note. She set it on the table on the bus feeling as if she'd put her heart into words and was about to leave it behind.

I did the best I could. This is yours. It always was. My signature below is my formal acknowledgement and agreement that I will never record or release this song in any way, shape, or form. I will never sue you for royalties or anything else for that matter. Record it with whoever you want. I just ask that you do not include my name anywhere on the release. Trace, you were right. Underneath all those muscles is a halfway decent guy. I hope you find him again.

Chaz Michaelson, the guy who's going to make sure they still remember my name tomorrow, is taking me back to Nashville and I've cleared my things off the bus. I'm keeping the gold dress from tonight, Pauly. You can bill me. Thanks for the ride boys—it was life changing as promised. Signed, Kylie Lou Ryans

Under the envelope she left Trace's blue plaid button up folded neatly. She hugged Carl on her way off the bus and he whispered good luck in her ear. She could hear Trace belting his friend Lee's song, *Hard to Love*, from inside the bar and it sounded like he was really giving it his all. Good for him. At the very least, maybe they'd both be a little stronger for having known each other.

chapter TWENTY NINE

"I CAN'T accept this, Kylie. It's sweet of you to offer, but it's too much." Tonya shoved the envelope back at her.

"Tonya, I'm almost positive he overpaid me." Probably out of guilt. "That's just the excess. I kept enough to pay first and last month's rent at my new place and kept a bit for some studio time at Bluebird. Clive made some calls so they're giving me a discounted rate."

"Kylie, you worked hard for this. You deserve it." Boy did she. But she wasn't taking Trace's guilt money, dammit. She could imagine how well that would go over, so instead of arguing with him, she would just put it to good use.

"If you hadn't suggested I change my song, none of this would've happened." On second thought, Kylie wondered if maybe she should be charging the woman for the years of gorging on mint chocolate chip it was going to take to get over what she'd been through. She sighed, trying not to think about it. She was fine, or at least she would be eventually. "And I left you high and dry with no one to help out. This should be enough for you to quit working weekends so you can be with your kiddo."

"Kylie..."

"Take the damn money, Tonya."

For a moment, neither of them spoke. Then Tonya rolled her eyes and held out her hand. "You'll never get anywhere in this business if you keep letting your emotions make all of your decisions."

“Thanks for the advice, cuz,” Kylie said, dropping the envelope into her friend’s hand. “Once again.” She smiled even though part of her felt guilty for not using it to buy her dad a headstone. But she knew he’d approve. And if everything went well and she was selected as the unsigned artist invited to join The Random Road Trip Tour, she would use that money to get her daddy the best headstone that money could buy.

“So Clive is riding everyone about this big birthday bash he’s throwing you. I swear, I’ve worked here two years and have never even gotten to take off on my birthday. You worked here two weeks and he acts like you’re his daughter or something.”

Kylie laughed. Maybe the old man could see that she needed someone to look out for her a little. “Don’t take it personal. He probably just knew a naïve hick from Oklahoma when he saw one.”

“Nah, Kylie, you’re a lot of things, but naïve isn’t one of them. In fact I was just thinking that you seem different, older somehow.”

Shrugging so her friend wouldn’t know how right she was, Kylie stood to leave. “Well, life on the road will age you.” She winked and said her goodbyes.

On her way out of the bar, her phone buzzed in the back pocket of her jeans. When Rae’s number and grinning face popped up on the screen, Kylie said a silent prayer. *Please let him be okay. Do not let this be a call telling me something bad has happened.*

“Hey Rae,” she answered.

“Kylieee!” Ray squealed. “How are you? How is recording going? I heard you were doing the Random Road Trip Tour and ohmygosh, I am totally coming to see you in Atlanta with all of my friends! Please tell me we can come back stage!”

“Um…” Kylie hesitated, unsure of which question to answer first. “I’m okay, just scheduled my recording time. Not entirely positive about the tour yet, but if I get on then yes you can.”

Rae laughed. “See, that’s why I love you. Trace would’ve just told me to slow down and ask one question at a time before he got a migraine!”

At the mention of his name, Kylie’s heart gave a little squeeze and made it hard to breathe normally. And then she was like an addict, ready to beg for more.

“Yeah, um, Rae? How is he? He’s not exactly speaking to me.”

“What? Oh no, so my acting skills didn’t help?” The girl sounded so dejected, Kylie was instantly overcome with guilt for burdening her with her problems.

"No, Rae, you did great. It's just…complicated." *I lied about having an evil stepmother, who is now blackmailing him, which he thinks I may be in on, got caught in a lie to get him where I wanted him, and now he hates me.* Okay, maybe it wasn't complicated, just screwed up and hopeless.

"Actually I haven't talked to him much either. He's been busy and hasn't been around much. But when I do, you want me to tell him you said hi?"

"Uh, no. That's okay, but thanks." Kylie fumbled her keys trying to hold the phone and unlock the door to her apartment at the same time. "Dammit."

"You okay?" Rae asked.

"Yeah I'm fine. Just dropped my keys."

"Okay, wellll," Rae drawled, "the reason I called is because my Sweet Sixteen party is tomorrow night and I would really love it if you could come, Kylie. The pool's open and we will probably have a bonfire and maybe dancing in the barn, kind of like Trace's party but minus the alcohol unfortunately. "

She couldn't help but laugh, and the invitation made her grin like an idiot. And then it made her want to cry. Because she couldn't go.

"Rae, I love you and I would love to come but—"

"Aw, Kylie. Please don't say no," Rae whined. "I know you're busy but geez, girl. Take a night off! You need to have some fun before you go on the road!"

Good point. And he might be there. Her hopes rose into her throat and then plummeted to her gut. That was exactly why she couldn't go. "Rae, I am going to send you an awesome present, I swear. And I am going to wish the coolest girl I know a happy birthday on Twitter and everywhere else, but like I said, Trace and I are not exactly on great terms right now and he was really mad about me using you to get him back to the bus the other night." Was that really just a week ago? Seemed like a lifetime. "Which I can see now I shouldn't have done, and I am truly sorry for asking you to lie like that," Kylie finished.

"Oh for crap's sake, he was acting like an idiot, and you were upset and worried about him. It's not like we lied to lure him into a sniper attack!"

Only Rae could make Kylie crack up in the middle of a conversation about something that had broken her heart. "True, but there's other stuff,

Rae, and it's just not a good situation right now."

"Because of the thing with your stepmom? That's what everyone is saying online, that you lied to seduce him and then you were going to sue or blackmail him or something."

Kylie's knees went weak as her stomach plummeted. "Please tell me that you and your family don't believe that," she choked out.

"No, of course we don't. And I don't think Trace does either…so what's the deal? Did you guys break up or what?"

"We weren't exactly *together*."

"Uh huh." Kylie could hear the girl smirking. "Really? 'Cause he's never brought a girl home to meet us, like ever, and he took you breakfast in bed and he hasn't done that since I was six and had the chicken pox and—"

"Rae, I get it. He's a nice guy, and I am so glad I got to know him and you and your family." *Even though missing all of you is killing me slowly and painfully right now.* "But I don't think he wants to see me and I know he doesn't want me at your party."

"Well then, it's a good thing he won't be there." Rae's voice was triumphant; this was her ace in the hole. "He's writing and recording up at his cabin. He told Claire Ann that he just couldn't get away this weekend, so he'll never even know."

"Rae…"

"Kyyylllliiiee…."

Kylie surveyed her empty apartment. She planned to run by a thrift store or some estate sales and get some furniture soon, but she hadn't yet. Ordering pizza in and sitting home alone versus hanging out with Rae and her friends at her favorite place in the whole world. Really wasn't much of contest. Even though the very sight of that place was going to carve another wound into her severed heart.

"Okay, Rae, I'll come," she relented. "What time and more importantly, what should I wear?"

Rae's answering shriek was almost deafening but Kylie was all smiles. Now she had to go shopping for something to wear and rent a car for the drive.

IT was a five-hour drive to Macon but Kylie needed the time to think, time to prepare herself for going back to the place where Trace Corbin had altered her irrevocably. Plus, she'd rented a bad ass Jeep Wrangler and rode with the top off for most of the way.

Her ponytail was a tangled mess but she was excited to see Rae. And the feeling was mutual. "Kylie! I'm so glad you made it!" Trace's younger sister greeted her with her typical enthusiasm.

Kylie had come early to help set up. After hugs from Rae and even Claire Ann, she busied herself with setting up tables in the barn to keep her mind off where she was. Not that the ragged hole in her chest was going to let her forget that easily.

"Just so you know," Trace's older sister began quietly as they lifted a round white table and shifted it towards the edge of the barn to make room for a dance floor. "We don't believe anything we hear from the media. If we did, we'd have disowned Trace long ago."

"I'm glad to hear it," Kylie told her, overcome with gratitude for Claire Ann's kind words. She was quiet and reserved and Kylie knew she didn't like to pry into Trace's life. "I would never hurt him, not intentionally," she swore.

"We know that. If anything, you helped him. The last few times we talked he seemed more focused on his career than he has ever been. And he's planning a big benefit to kick off some program he's working on to help out single working parents."

Kylie's whole body went weak at the woman's words. "He is?"

He'd read her lyrics about Tonya, and they'd talked about the unfairness of her dad trying to go it alone after her mom died. He'd really been listening.

"Yeah, but missing Rae's birthday is going to land him in the hot seat with her no matter how many charities he sponsors." Claire Ann was smiling but Kylie couldn't return it.

When Trace's sister saw Kylie's eyes filling with tears, she promptly lowered the table and stepped around it. "Kylie, I don't know what's going on with you two, and frankly, it's really none of my business so I'm not going to ask. But why don't you go on inside and freshen up? You've had a long drive. I'll tell Rae you'll be out in a little while."

Kylie sucked in a breath and dammed up her tears. "I swear I am not this girl. I don't get all weepy over some guy. I don't know what's the matter with me. Just being here with all of you and missing him and—"

"Shh, I understand. Things will work out however they are meant to. Sometimes we all just need a little time. Trace has never been very good at talking about his feelings or hammering things out. He just…well, you know."

"Yeah," Kylie whispered. "Thanks. I think I'll go inside and clean up a bit."

GOING into the house where she'd made love to Trace was a horrible idea. Good call, Claire Ann.

Kylie took a quick shower in Trace's master bath, trying to keep the images of what had happened last time she was in there out of her mind. It wasn't really working. Especially since the shower door bar she'd broken was lying on the side of the tub screaming "exhibit A" at her.

After she'd cleaned up and put on the short peachy-pink belted dress she'd bought, she slipped on her boots and decided to let her hair air dry out in the Georgia heat. No more crying, she promised herself. It was Rae's night and she wasn't going to ruin it by acting like a lovesick idiot. Even if she was one.

Most of the party had arrived by the time Kylie walked out to the pool. A flash of being thrown into the pond farther out on the property threatened to crash into her, but she held it off. Some annoyingly catchy pop song blared from a radio nearby and the sounds of laughter and splashing reminded Kylie that she was here to have fun.

Striding purposefully over to sit by Rae, she glanced around. Several girls were in bikinis and a few were dressed like her. Most of the guys were in swim trunks. A couple of each were giving her some serious side-eye but mostly they just kept goofing around in the pool. Being friends with Trace Corbin's little sister probably required a good bit of discretion. But someone had leaked information about her last visit here so she was wary. Kylie slipped her feet out of her boots and sat them next to her.

"So which boy is the one you like?" she whispered as she lowered herself to the slate surrounding the pool and dipped her feet in the cool water.

"Teal Hollister trunks," Rae whispered back.

"Ah, very cute." Kylie smiled and nodded her approval. Lulu would like Rae very much. The thought of them all hanging out made Kylie smile.

"What?" Rae asked, leaning away from her. "Don't be hitting on my man, Kylie Ryans. I'm serious."

At that Kylie burst out laughing. "I wouldn't dream of it, Rae. But I was thinking, now you have to come to Nashville next Monday for my birthday. My best friend Lulu is coming up from our hometown and we're going out dancing. Think Claire Ann might come too?"

"Um, hell yes!" Rae squealed, giving Kylie a damp hug. "And I promise, I won't tell Trace."

"You promise you won't tell Trace what?" his voiced boomed from behind them.

Kylie squeezed her eyes shut as her insides slid to the tips of her toes. She wondered for a second if she'd been set up, but she could tell from the way Rae leapt into his arms that it was a surprise to both of them.

"Trace," she said evenly as she stood to face him, ignoring the dizziness threatening to knock her back down.

"Kylie?" The surprise on his face said he wasn't expecting to see her any more than she had been planning to see him.

"Rae said you weren't coming, so I—"

"And now my two favorite people are here and we're going to have so much fun!" Rae chirped. Kylie knew she was trying to dispel the awkwardness of the situation. Bless her heart.

"You didn't really think I'd miss your birthday, did you?" Trace asked, turning from Kylie to Rae. God, why did he have to be so damned handsome? He looked like he hadn't shaved in a week and aviator sunglasses hid his eyes, but the man was practically radiating hotness in front of the setting sun. She slipped back into her boots, readying herself to make a quick getaway. Every beat of her heart was taking twice the usual effort.

"I know you've been busy," Rae answered with a shrug.

"Never too busy for you, darlin'." Trace kissed his little sister on the head. Kylie's body shifted into fight or flight mode. The way he'd said darlin' to Rae was the same way he'd said it to her. *Flight. Definitely flight.*

"Rae, I'm gonna grab your present and then I'm gonna head on back. It's a long drive. 'Scuse me."

Kylie walked as quickly as possible to the barn where she'd parked her jeep. She thought she heard someone say her name but she kept going. No way she could turn back now.

"ARE you trying to turn my family against me?"

Just as Kylie leaned over the front seat of the jeep to grab Rae's present, she heard Trace's warm voice and frigid words.

"What?" she asked, grabbing the gift and turning to face him.

"What are you doing here?"

"Rae invited me. I tried to turn her down but she's…persistent." *And now I look like an idiot and like I'm stalking you, just like the media says.*

"Yeah, I know she is," he said, stuffing his hands into the pockets of his jeans.

"Anyways, she said you wouldn't be here so I came but now you're here and I'm going to give her this and go." Kylie slammed the Jeep door shut and started to walk past him but he reached out an arm and then dropped it before touching her.

For a second he just stared at it, like it had betrayed him somehow. But then he looked up and slid off his glasses. Tired eyes ringed with dark circles stared her down warily. "You drove here from Nashville?"

"I did." Kylie clutched the gift, grateful to have something to hold onto.

"Why?"

Kylie huffed out a sigh. She so did not want to do this now. This was Rae's party. "Because I needed time to think. And I could just imagine what the media would say if it leaked that I bought a plane ticket to your hometown."

"How thoughtful of you," Trace sneered as if he didn't really believe her.

"Yeah, well, underneath all this spray tan is a halfway decent girl, believe it or not." Kylie hadn't meant to throw his words back at him like that but there it was.

"Look," he began, pulling off his baseball cap and running a hand through his hair before replacing it. "I've worked extremely hard to keep my shitty life choices from affecting them, so I'd appreciate it if you would just steer clear of my family altogether. Please." His tone wasn't hateful. It sounded like he was pleading with her actually, but his words jabbed and stung in all her weakest places. He'd called her a shitty life choice.

"Got it. Here." Kylie shoved the Tiffany's box at him and turned back to her Jeep. "Tell Rae I'm sorry."

"Kylie, wait. I didn't mean—"

But she didn't hear the rest of whatever he had to say. She'd already slammed the door to the Jeep and was starting it up. *Do not peel out. Do not act like a psycho. Just leave calmly and do not ever, EVER come back.*

OVER the next few days, Rae launched an attack on Kylie's phone via text messages. *Where did you go? What happened? I didn't know he was coming, I swear. Please don't be mad at me. Am I still invited next week? Kylie, I know he's an ass but he just wasn't expecting to see you. I am very mad at him but he bought me a car so I have forgiven him. ;) Please, please call me so we can talk.*

Kylie deleted each and every one of them without responding. She would not keep doing this to all of them. They were Trace's family and he thought of her as just another shitty life choice he'd made, one that just wouldn't take the hint and go away. She wished she could make herself think of him the same way.

chapter THIRTY ONE

"I NEED you to meet me at 5:15 on Monday morning, Kylie. I know it's early but my schedule is packed full and I need you to sign these releases like yesterday. I'll buy you breakfast," Trace's manager promised.

Yeah it was early. And it was her damned birthday. Not that anyone really cared. Though Lulu and her cousin Carmen were coming to see her. She tried to tell herself it was because they wanted to and not just because she'd bought them plane tickets and insisted that they do so.

"Pauly, you have the note," she told him with a sigh. "I spelled it out and signed."

"I know. And I swear that's good enough for me, but the label wants that to be the next song Trace releases and they won't let him record it until they have the official papers on file."

Oh. Ouch. She hadn't realized he would record it so soon.

"Um, who's he planning to record it with?" she asked, not really sure if she wanted to know the answer.

"I don't really know for sure. Lots of names have been mentioned," he told her, sounding more than a little uncomfortable.

"Okay, Pauly. 5:15 in the freaking morning on my friggin' birthday. Meet you at Eggcetera and you *will* buy me breakfast," she told him before hanging up. Something that had been lying dormant since the tour had ended stirred in her. The memory of her telling Trace about her dad's birthday tradition made its way to the surface of her thoughts.

Pauly had made a point of telling her once that he didn't get involved in Trace's personal life, but maybe this time he'd made an exception. Maybe Trace had set this up so that they could have breakfast together on her birthday. *Shitty life choice, Kylie. That's what he considers you.*

Surely Pauly didn't actually want her to sign some stupid papers before sun up. At the very least, Trace might want to talk things out so they could have some type of friendship. The truth was, she hoped so. Because she missed him. Missed him so much she felt hollow and empty without him.

SHE jolted awake at 5:15 to the sound of her phone ringing. Pauly was on her caller ID. But she was still holding out hope that maybe it was Trace. Either way she was already late. *Shit.*

She jumped off the couch, splashed her face with cold water, and took a swig of mouth wash. After pulling her hair into a ponytail, she threw on some clean-ish jeans and her Charlie Daniels Band t-shirt. She full out sprinted to Eggcetera. Where Pauly was waiting and tapping his watch. Her heart sank into her stomach. It was just him.

"Hey, it's my birthday, Pauly. Give a girl a break." She glanced around, hoping to see Trace somewhere nearby but she didn't. Because he wasn't there. *Of course he isn't.*

"Yeah, yeah. Happy birthday, kid," he said with a smirk. Wow, so this was her big birthday morning. A grumbly manager, who wasn't even hers, buying her breakfast in a greasy diner. Quite a change from her dad making pancakes and singing to her. *Welcome to being a grown up.*

"Okay," Pauly began, laying out several papers in front of her. "This first one says that you relinquish all rights to Trace of the song you co-wrote entitled *The Other Side of Me*, the second one says that you understand that you will not receive any formal acknowledgment or royalties from the song, and the third one says that you will not ever try to release the song as your own even under a different title. Those are for the label. This fourth one is for me and it's a standard non-disclosure agreement regarding your relationship with Trace and any contact you have had with him up to this point. It states that you will not ever discuss the nature of your interaction with him during the tour or otherwise. You with me, Kylie?"

Good morning, Pauly. How are you? Me? I'm fabulous, thanks for asking.

"Yeah, just, um, I need a pen." J*ust sign the dotted line and erase yourself from his life forever*. Got it.

"Kylie," Pauly huffed as he handed her a pen. "You need to sit here and read these carefully before you sign."

"I trust you, Pauly," she told him as she began to sign the first line with the X by it. "And I trust Trace, too," she added quietly. Trusted that he wanted her out of his life bad enough to make it official.

"Now you listen to me, Kylie Ryans," Pauly said, snatching the pen from her hand. "You trust no one, do you understand? I work for Trace, and other managers work for their artists, and do not ever for one second think that just because someone likes you they won't trick you into signing something that could be damaging to you. Matter of fact, from now on you take Chaz or an attorney with you any time you are asked to sign anything." The manager leaned forward and held her gaze until she responded.

"Pauly, it's five-thirty in the morning, and honestly, there's really no way Trace could hurt me more than he already has. Do you want me to sign the damn papers or not?" Kylie was way past out of patience. She couldn't wait for this to be over so she could snuggle down in her bed until it was time to pick up her friends at the airport. Thank God she'd finally be recording in the studio tomorrow. She had a lot of pain and anguish to work out.

Pauly sighed and handed her the heavy black pen back. "Okay, but I mean it. From here on out you read anything you sign and get Chaz and a lawyer to read it too."

"Yes, Dad," she said without thinking. She scribbled her name across all the papers and grabbed a menu. "So what are you having?" she asked the man staring at his phone instead of a menu.

"Actually I've got another meeting I have to get to but I've already told the waitress I'm covering your breakfast, so order anything you like." Pauly gathered the signed documents and slid them into a folder.

"You're not staying?" She tried to keep the pathetic whine of abandonment out of her voice. Fail.

"Happy birthday, Kylie. And good luck with Vitamin Water thing," the manager said as he slid out of the booth.

"How did you—"

"Small town." He answered her unfinished question just before he turned on his heel and left. Geez, she'd just now heard about it being a real possibility in a text from Chaz. She should be excited. But after signing legal documents reminding her that she no longer had any connection to Trace Corbin, she couldn't muster even an ounce of enthusiasm.

When the waitress came she ordered a coffee to go and rested her head on her table while she waited. Even after everything with Trace, she'd never felt more used and alone than right that moment.

Carrying her Styrofoam cup of coffee up the stairs to her apartment was nearly impossible. Because she was made of lead and the small cup of coffee weighed at least a hundred pounds. She missed her dad. Just thinking about him stung her deep inside because she knew he'd be disappointed in her.

The daughter he'd raised never would've let her feelings over some ridiculous man keep her from focusing on her career. Lifting her head as she trudged up the stairs, she vowed to stop this stupidity. She was not this girl. Coming to Nashville had been her dream because she loved the gift of music her father had given her and damned if she wasn't going to use it.

Glancing at her watch as she reached her door, she realized it was 5:40. Two minutes past when her dad would've barged into her room with his guitar. She took a deep breath and wiped her face hard to keep the tears from coming.

The smell of pancakes and bacon thick in the air made Kylie wonder if she was hallucinating. Most likely it just clung to her from the diner. Now if she saw her dad come through the apartment singing Happy Birthday and holding his guitar, she was going to need to see a shrink, and soon.

But when she opened the door to her apartment, that's exactly what she saw.

WHEN the man in front of her stopped singing, Kylie used every ounce of strength she had to stay vertical. It wasn't easy since her legs were ready to give out and leave her slumping against the door.

"What are you doing here? How did you even get in?" she asked, clutching her cup of coffee so tightly she worried she'd puncture it.

"Word on the street is that you're having a rough time, and I, uh, have friends in high places," he said with a wink.

"Oh yeah? Well, I don't need your pity party, Trace Corbin," she said through gritted teeth.

"That's not the only reason," he told her, setting down her guitar and taking off his hat.

"I'm listening."

Trace cleared his throat and leaned against the breakfast bar. "What you said on the bus, I didn't mean to make you feel that way." She could see the strain in his eyes but she was also hearing what he wasn't saying. Pity and guilt—that's why he was here.

"And how did you think it would make me feel, being compared to Darla, called a lying whore, and getting kicked out of Rae's birthday party?" Her heart pounded so forcefully against her chest she was sure it was visible through her shirt.

"You take that saying everything you feel real seriously, don't you?" Trace inquired as he pulled his hat back on.

"You know I do." *And he knew why.* Kylie clenched her fists. She'd never wanted to strike another human being as badly as she wanted to hit Trace Corbin right that second.

"Well then here's one for you. After learning that you lied about not having any living relatives when we'd slept together, I was angry and pretty damn afraid that you were part of some grand scheme to end my career. But when I heard you telling Cora on Skype that it was a one-time thing, well that felt even shittier than being lied to."

Something hard in her softened a few degrees. "What was I supposed to think, Trace? You paid off my stepmother, for which I was about to thank you when you burst in and called me a no talent hack who no one would remember." She shrugged but her vital organs seemed to be struggling to function, squeezing and clenching and thudding inside of her.

"Kylie, all I can say is that I am a different man when I've been drinking and not a particularly good one. I say things I don't mean and then don't remember saying them. My dad…well, he was like that too. Trust me when I say it's not something I'm proud of. But what I said about your career after the, er, encounter with your stepmom was just me repeating to Pauly the lies I told her to make her go the hell away. I'd hoped it would be enough to get her out of your life for good."

"Okay, well, that does make me feel better," she told him, setting her coffee down on the counter. "But you also called me a shitty life choice when you were completely sober, and frankly, you were probably right."

"Kylie…"

"No, just, no," she said, shaking her head to keep him from continuing. "I don't know what you're really doing here or what came over us after your party but I know that things would be better if we'd never met." Kylie sucked in a breath, ignoring the way he recoiled at her harsh words, and continued. "You've taken everything good in my life and turned it into something painful. I should be on cloud freaking nine right now but all I do is miss you and hurt. My whole life I wanted to be touring and recording music with people who give a damn about me, and my career and now my dreams are finally coming true. But all I feel is emptiness because I'm wishing I was on a farm in Georgia with someone who considers me nothing more than a shitty life choice." Her head kept turning slightly back and forth as if she were disagreeing with her own words. Or maybe it was because she couldn't believe she was saying them, out loud, to the one person she didn't want to tell.

Trace huffed out a breath and stared at her for what felt like forever. His forehead scrunched as if he were deciding whether or not to divulge a precious secret. "That's not what I meant," he said evenly with a slight shake of his own head. "I wasn't talking about you when I said that, but I knew how it sounded and I tried to apologize and explain, but you left... and Kylie, what you just said, about people giving a damn? I hate to be the one to tell you this, but no one really does. This is a business and that's all. You'll save yourself a hell of a lot of hurt and disappointment if you realize that now."

He said something else but all she heard was *I don't give a damn about you—no one really does.*

"Thank you for the life lessons, Trace. Please go now." She swallowed hard and squeezed her eyes shut. No way she would have the strength to let him go any other way. She couldn't keep looking at the blue shirt he wore. It was the same damn one of his that was supposed to be hers. All he wanted was to keep schooling her about the gritty underbelly of the business or whatever, and all she wanted was him.

"Okay, I'll go," he said, barely above a whisper. "But you asked why I came and I never got to answer. I came to tell you I'm sorry for the things I've said and done that have hurt you, truly I am. I care about you, Kylie, and any guy who only wants you for one night is a damned fool."

A tiny squeak escaped her throat at Trace's words.

"And you're not the only one that would give it all up to go back to that day in Macon. Bye, Kylie Lou. You take care of yourself." He stepped closer, looming over her as she shrunk beneath his words. *Say something. Ask him to stay. Tell him you care about him right back.* But he kissed her on the top of her head and let himself out. Time stood still around her as she took in the pancakes and bacon Trace had made sitting on the counter.

It was enough to convince her legs to finally give out beneath her. That was twice now that a man she loved reached out and she let him go. Like in her nightmares, she just couldn't find the words.

"I'M so excited to see you, Kylie! Carmen is, too!" Lulu was practically squealing from the speaker in Kylie's phone.

"Yeah, Lu, I'm excited too." But her voice gave her away. She was struggling to get excited about much of anything lately. She hadn't told her friend a whole lot about the situation with Trace. She didn't want to relay the details only for Carmen to ask her what she was going to do next, because Kylie had no answer for that. "Have to say, kind of surprised that Carmen is excited to see me." Kylie and Lulu's cousin had never really been the best of friends. Not that Kylie was really in a position to turn down friends at this point. Trace was definitely right about one thing—this lifestyle could be lonely.

"Of course she is! And she's excited to see Nashville." Yeah, that made more sense. "Okay, our flight is boarding. See you in a few hours!"

"Great," Kylie agreed, forcing herself to exert the proper amount of enthusiasm for her friend's visit. "And when do you have to go back?"

"I have classes tomorrow morning so we're taking the red eye back tonight."

"Okay, well, I'll grab a cab and meet you in a bit."

KYLIE almost didn't recognize Lulu when she got off the plane. Her hair had been a bright shade of pink on their last Skype chat and now it was white blond with lower tips tinged with magenta. Carmen looked the same but she was smiling instead of scowling, which made her look a whole lot prettier than Kylie remembered.

She wrapped her best friend in a tight hug. "Hey, hot mama. Love the hair."

"Oh em gee, it's Kiii Lee Ryans!" Lulu squealed.

Several people turned to look at them. "God, shut up, Lu," Kylie said with a laugh as she met Carmen's eyes and they shared an eye roll. Man, she'd missed this crazy girl.

After they got some food and were back at Kylie's apartment, she filled them in on everything from the night she met Trace at The Rum Room to their encounter this morning. She left out the intimate details about the day after his party but they got the idea.

"Damn," Carmen said, letting out a low whistle, "that's harsh."

"I am so going to junk punch Trace Corbin. Where does he live?" Lulu demanded. "And I am posting his real name online. Tracey Corbin has a nicer ring to it, and now he can do a drag show."

Kylie sighed. She didn't have the emotional energy necessary to get angry. Thankfully Lulu had enough for both of them. "I think he just wants to put everything that happened behind him and it's kind of hard to do that if I show up at his house and hang out with his sisters."

"Well, what the hell ever. That's no way to treat you. It's not like you even actually lied to him. You just didn't mention it. I mean, since when do people have to fill out a family tree to get a job?"

"They asked me in the initial interview if I had any skeletons in my closet, anything that might cause problems for Trace," Kylie said quietly. "I lied because it seemed like any sign of drama might cause them to change their minds. I'm lucky it wasn't worse than this."

"Worse than this? Kylie, your freaking dreams are coming true and you're just sitting here lonely and heartbroken, and don't deny it. I can see what this has done to you."

"So can I," Carmen added quietly.

"Well, that can't be helped," she snapped without meaning to. Softer she added, "I just wish I'd told him about her, that day on the farm. But it is what it is and the media has turned it into something ugly and…" Kylie just shook her head, unable to finish.

"And he's acting like a teenage dickhead who screws girls and tosses them aside when it's no longer convenient. And then what the hell did he really want this morning? A quickie?"

"I don't think so." Kylie closed her eyes and tried to put what she believed into words. "He's trying to rebuild his image. You know how country music is—wholesome, moral, down home values and all that. He's made a lot of mistakes and here he was trying to start from the ground up and I come along and now all anyone can talk about is him hooking up with some girl whose own mother has labeled her a gold-digging whore." She cringed on the last part. That was worst thing about the whole ordeal—no one seemed to care that Darla was just her *step*mother. The leaks about interviews with Darla kept calling her Kylie's mother. Made Kylie's stomach turn. Hard.

"Yeah, but it's not like you planned it and seduced him or anything. He's a consenting adult for crying out loud," Lu argued.

"And even if you did, it's not like you've done anything to really hurt him. Or sold everything you learned about him to some cheap tabloid. What's the big damned deal?" Carmen added.

"I think it's that, in this business, it's hard to trust people. I mean, I've been really lucky, but I know Trace had some shady characters lying to him and manipulating him when he first started out." Sadness and regret washed over her, threatening to keep her from continuing. She took a deep breath and hurried on. "He mentioned some things and his sister told me some stuff. I think it really hurt him that he trusted me and I lied…or that I didn't tell him the truth before things went as far as they did. When I had Rae lie to get him back to the bus—that just sent him over the edge. Then he walked up on us talking about her promising not to tell him something at her party. Just, *ugh*. If our relationship or whatever it was had a theme, it would be bad timing."

For a moment no one said anything. Carmen was on the couch. Kylie and Lulu sat on the floor propped against it. CMT was on but the volume was down too low to be audible.

Kylie stared at her hands and swallowed back tears. She had been looking forward to Lu's visit and now she was ruining it with a pity party. They were supposed to be going shopping and then to dinner before her party at The Rum Room, not listening to her sulk in her scarcely furnished apartment. Taking a deep breath, she started to open her mouth to tell the girls, her friends, that it was just over and that they should all just drop it and enjoy tonight. But Lulu spoke first.

"Well, speak of the devil. Turn it up, Carmen."

Kylie looked at the television she'd bought at the pawnshop near her apartment. And there he was. Wearing a grin worthy of swooning girls everywhere.

Our own Mandy Lynn Mathis caught up with Trace Corbin as he prepares for the upcoming Workin' Hard Lovin' Harder benefit concert. The camera panned to a tall blonde woman holding a microphone and standing with Trace in what looked like a giant auditorium. Kylie couldn't breathe. *A shitty life choice. That's what you are to him.* The TV drowned out her inner monologue.

Trace Corbin, fresh off his Back to My Roots tour is gearing up to perform at a benefit concert at The Sommet Center next month to help raise money for a charity he's just started. Trace, can you tell us a little about this program and your involvement?

Yes, ma'am. Recently I was made aware of the difficulties that single parents face. Particularly ones who have to sacrifice time with their children working multiple jobs to make ends meet. After my father passed, my own mama raised my little sister all on her own. All of the money we raise tonight will go to A HAND UP, *which is a foundation my family and I have started to help single working parents locate safe and affordable housing and childcare. It will also help with bills, groceries, and any medical or other costs they may incur.* Even Mandy Lynn Mathis looked surprised. How long had he been working on this? Kylie wondered as she stared at the screen.

Trace, that's really noble of you. What do you say to your critics out there who say you're just doing this to cover all the negative publicity you received on this last tour?

Well, Ms. Mathis, frankly I don't much care about my critics. My focus is on my family and my fans. The people who've stuck with me when I least deserved it.

Good for you, Trace. Any chance you care to tell us about the multiple opening acts you worked with on this tour?

Um, yeah. Sure. Kylie watched Trace shift his weight. *We had some great artists along for the ride, some of which didn't work out, as you know, but we had a great time on the road, and we're all really grateful to everyone who came to see us play.*

Now Trace, we've heard rumors about missed tour dates, and it's been said that your manager even went on the road with you to make sure you showed up to each and every show. Any truth to that?

Nah, Pauly just loves my company. Trace laughed but Kylie knew it wasn't his real laugh.

Well that's understandable, the woman said with a wink. Ugh, the freaking CMT correspondent was flirting with him. Kylie was so never going to let that woman interview her.

Okay, one last question before we let you get back to rehearsing. Mia Montgomery and Kylie Ryans were both talented young ladies who toured with you briefly. Rumors are still circulating about the nature of your relationships with each. Care to clear the air?

Trace slid off his hat and ran a hand through his hair. Kylie recognized the gesture. He was nervous.

Country music fans have certain expectations. Mia Montgomery was a pop crossover artist who had recently come off a tour for a contest she won. She wasn't well received by audiences who had bought a ticket to see a country concert. She left the tour early to work on her kind of music. To my knowledge there were no hard feelings.

And Ms. Ryans? the correspondent prompted.

The little volume squares appeared as Carmen turned the flat screen clear up to sonic boom. Trace's voice filled the apartment as the three girls watched with wide eyes.

He cleared his throat before he spoke directly into the camera. *Kylie Ryans is an extremely strong and talented young woman whose only flaw was to have the sheer misfortune of getting stuck on a bus with me.* Trace forced another chuckle that Kylie knew wasn't genuine. *She's a stick of dynamite. I'm expecting great things to happen for her and I wish her the best. At the rate she's going, I'll probably be opening for her in a year or so.* He grinned but the smile didn't reach his eyes.

Thanks, Trace. Best of luck with your upcoming concert and A Hand Up.

Thank you. Trace dipped his head towards the woman and then he disappeared from the frame as the camera zoomed in on Mandy Lynn Mathis.

And for those of you not in attendance, you can watch Trace perform live on CMT on Demand from—

The apartment went silent as Carmen hit mute.

The only thing Kylie could hear was the blood rushing in her ears. An echo of Trace's words began to rise above the fluid.

"Well, maybe I won't junk punch him, but I am going to call him Tracey. Loudly. In public," Lulu announced.

"Why would he…just…he didn't…" Kylie couldn't form a coherent thought to save her life. Tears blurred her vision and she could feel herself shaking.

"Carmen, check the freezer for ice cream, and if there isn't any, run down the street to that little store we passed on the way in and buy some. Mint chocolate chip. Get the big bucket," Lulu ordered. Carmen snapped to attention and was out the door.

"Why would he say those things? After…" After she'd shoved him out of her life to protect herself from what she knew they were capable of doing to each other.

"Oh, honey." Lulu wrapped Kylie in a hug and held her while she cried out all of the tears she had left for Trace Corbin.

"COME on, Kylie! We're going to be late! Hurry the hell up!" Lulu banged on the bathroom door.

Kylie stepped out of the bathroom wrapped in her towel. She knew she was going to run a little late to her own birthday party, but it had taken a while to figure out what to do.

She was going to hope and pray that Trace came to her party tonight, that they could talk. And if he didn't show, she was going to call him and ask him to meet her for coffee or something. She was ready. Ready to apologize for not telling him about Darla when he'd been so honest about his family situation. Ready to do whatever it took to convince him that she cared about him too and that even if he thought he couldn't do relationships, she wanted him to try. With her. Her heartbeat sped up each time she thought about him, about what it would feel to kiss him again, and to be in his arms where she belonged.

"So I've got good news and bad news," Lulu announced as she passed Kylie to get into the bathroom and plug up the hair straightener. "Good news is I forgot to tell you that there's a giant billboard up at home that says Pride is Proud of Kylie Ryans." The kindness of the town that Kylie had deserted made her eyes moist. Maybe she did have some semblance of a family after all.

"And the bad news?"

Lulu stepped back towards the bed and picked up her cell phone.

"E!Online has started a poll: Kylie Ryans, Starlet or Harlot? People are voting and commenting like crazy."

"Well, what's the verdict?"

Lulu checked her phone. "It's tied dead even at fifty percent for each."

"Fabulous."

"This is the kind of dress that changes your life, Ky. You have to wear it tonight," Lulu told her, changing the subject by holding up the tiny black strapless dress she'd talked Kylie into purchasing earlier that afternoon when they'd been out shopping.

"Not sure I can handle too many more life changing experiences," Kylie told her as she eyed it warily.

"Sure you can, and these shoes are perfect." She gestured to the black stilettos Kylie would never be able to walk in.

"Yeah, perfect for busting my ass."

"Nah, you'll be fine. Practice walking in them till it's time to go."

"Hey, Kylie. There's, um, a delivery for you," Carmen called from the front of the apartment.

"Okay," Kylie called back, looking down at her towel and stilettos. "Lu, you wanna get that for me?"

Lulu just rolled her eyes and darted towards the door to see what had arrived.

"Um, Ky, I think you're going to want to see this," she called a few seconds later. Kylie wobbled on her heels as she made her way out of the bedroom. And her breath caught in her throat.

In her living room stood Rae and Claire Ann Corbin.

Kylie wondered briefly if the entire Corbin family met privately to discuss these sneak attacks they were so damned good at.

"What are you guys doing here?" she asked, trying to sound happy to see them. Wasn't too hard because she was.

"Surprise!" Rae shouted.

"Crashing your birthday," Claire Ann answered quietly. Kylie laughed. And then she introduced everyone.

"It's Olivia, actually," Lulu corrected after Kylie introduced her. Apparently she was going with her more adult name, not that Kylie would ever be able to call her by it.

"Whatever," Kylie said with an eye roll. "Don't get me wrong, I'm beyond happy to see y'all but, um, Trace—"

"Trace is kind of an ass sometimes, Kylie. Surely you've noticed?" Claire Ann asked.

"Amen, sister," Lulu chimed in.

"Hey, is that what you're wearing tonight because, um…" Rae trailed off, taking in Kylie's robe and heels.

"Yes, Rae. This step one of my five-point plan to get your brother to fall in love with me," Kylie deadpanned.

"Oh, nice." Rae nodded as if she thought it was a step in the right direction. "Well, what's step two?"

"Yeah, I haven't really gotten that far yet," Kylie told her.

"Looking hot should pretty much do it," Lulu chimed in. "Which she totally is. Wait till y'all see the dress she's wearing tonight."

And with that, everyone began comparing outfits, critiquing and clamoring over each other to make suggestions about how she should wear her hair.

This is what it must be like to have sisters, Kylie thought to herself. And at that moment, with Carmen turning up the radio, Lulu helping her put her dress on without getting deodorant on it, Claire Ann heating up the hair straightener, and Rae digging through her makeup, Kylie thought that other than being with Trace, this was probably about as good as it ever got.

"Good God, Kylie. The rest of us might as well wear paper sacks," Carmen blurted out once they were all dressed. She blushed at the unexpected compliment.

"No shit," Lulu added. "Trace Corbin must be a blind idi—" She covered her mouth and glanced at Rae and Claire Ann. "Crap, sorry."

Rae burst out in laughter and Claire Ann shook her head. "Agreed," Rae said with a grin at Kylie.

chapter THIRTY FIVE

THE Rum Room was packed when the girls arrived. They'd walked from Kylie's apartment and her "killer heels," as Lulu called them, were in fact killing her already. But once she stepped into the warm open bar with its pulsing blare of drums and bass and thick smell of cologne and liquor, budding excitement electrified her insides. Maybe this would be a really fun night after all.

"Ahh! The birthday girl is here!" Kylie heard a familiar voice shout over the music.

"Tonya! What are you doing working tonight? I thought you told Clive no more weekends?"

"I did and I normally just work Tuesday through Thursday now, and no more late nights, thank you very much. But I couldn't miss a chance to see you and get paid to do it! And Clive knew your party would draw a crowd so he's paying me double to work overtime."

"Think he'll let you have a drink with us? Coke for me. I'm still underage you know," Kylie whispered conspiratorially as her friends pulled her deeper into the thick crowd.

"Yeah, probably," Tonya answered with a laugh. "And I might even be able to slip some rum into that Coke," she teased. A few minutes after Tonya had disappeared into the crowd, Clive himself made his way over to Kylie's table.

She introduced him to her friends and Trace's sisters, who she had decided were going into her friend category whether he liked it or not.

"You know, if I wasn't so damn proud of you, I'd be pissed that you left without giving notice," he said as he gave her a big sweaty hug.

"Don't worry, Clive. My music career will probably be over soon and I'll be back here waiting tables in no time."

"I seriously doubt that, young lady, but you are welcome anytime. Speaking of which, I was kind of hoping you might sing a few songs for us tonight if you don't mind."

"Mind? I'd be honored. And seriously, I'm sorry about ditching you, Clive. All I can say is I had nothing, and this was my dream, to work here, play music here, and now my dreams are running away with me."

"Listen, that's life. We make our own luck and you put all you had into something and it's paying off. I couldn't be more proud if you were my own daughter."

Clive's kind words had her old friend, the throat lump of tears to come, threatening to surface, but she shook it off.

"Thank you. That means more than you know."

"You just enjoy your night and if you get the urge to sing, I'll kick those yahoos off and the stage is all yours. Your bill is on the house tonight. Happy birthday, young lady," he said just before ambling off to speak with some men who'd just walked in.

"Let's go, girl! Time to party!" Lulu shouted and Rae whistled in agreement. Claire Ann sat in a booth near the dance floor and watched them all acting silly. Kylie knew the twenty-eight year old had mainly just come to escort Rae but she couldn't help but wish she'd loosen up a little. After a few minutes Kylie dragged her onto the floor.

And Claire Ann had some moves. *It's always the quiet ones*, Kylie thought to herself.

After dancing themselves sweaty, the girls headed to the booth where Clive had hung a picture of Kylie and Trace singing that first night and a framed napkin Kylie recognized as the one she'd signed for Tonya.

The photo made her stomach clench in anticipation, so Kylie told them she'd get some waters from the bar.

Just as she managed to arrange five bottled waters in her hands, Kylie turned towards her booth. But her path was blocked. By a crowd of people gathering to gawk at some guy and his date. *Geez people. Get a grip.* As she stepped around the crowd, she got a look at who was causing all the fuss.

Trace Corbin had just finished signing autographs and pulling out a seat for his date. A tall brunette with olive skin lowered her perfect red silk covered frame into the chair Trace held out for her. Kylie recognized the woman. Mia Montgomery.

"Here," Kylie said setting the waters on Tonya's tray as she started to walk past. "I can't," was all she could get out.

"No prob, I'll take them to—" Tonya broke off as she took in Kylie's blank expression. "Kylie, what's the matter?" The waitress followed her friend's line of sight. "Oh."

"I'll take that rum and Coke now. Please," Kylie whispered.

"Kylie—"

"Please, Tonya," she begged, not taking her eyes off the couple that seemed to be oblivious to all the attention they were getting.

A few seconds or an hour might've passed, she wasn't sure. But her friend finally returned to where she stood, hidden behind the growing cluster of patrons at the bar.

"Here. It's a double so—" Tonya didn't finish her warning because Kylie had already downed the contents of the glass.

The burn jolted her back to life. *Get the hell out of here before anyone sees you freaking out.*

Kylie mumbled a thanks to her friend and darted stealthily back to her table.

"Hey, um, so that happened," she told the group as she gestured to Trace and Mia sitting in the middle of the room.

"What the hell is he doing here?" Rae and Lulu blurted almost in unison.

"We have to get out of here now," Kylie said, barely resisting the urge to run out with or without them. "I wish I was some badass that could go over there and act all cool about this but I'm not and I can't."

"Okay, let's go," Lulu said, sliding out of the booth quickly as she recognized Kylie's *I'm about to lose my shit and cry all over the place* face.

"Seriously, Kylie? You're going to let him run you out of your own party? Nashville isn't that big. Y'all are bound to run into each other from time to time," Carmen criticized matter-of-factly.

"She's kind of right you know," Rae added softly. "I know he ran you out of my party, and if you keep running eventually you're going to let him run you right out of your career."

Kylie glanced at her friends, Lulu standing next to her and the other three sitting and waiting for her to suck it up. Then she glanced at the door. Exhaling most of the tension from her chest, she plopped down into the booth. "I thought I could keep them separate," she announced quietly to no one in particular. "My feelings for Trace and my feelings for music." She shook her head at her own stupidity as the girls around her leaned in to listen. Lulu scooted closer than necessary. "I can't. They're the same thing," she finished quietly.

For a moment no one said anything. Then Carmen, of all people, spoke. "Kylie, if it makes you feel any better, it's very obvious that they're here to be seen. They're like posing for pictures with fake-ass smiles all over the place." She nodded at the couple and Kylie saw them doing exactly as she said. It did help a little.

"Okay, well let's just chill over here until he leaves." Hopefully that would be sooner rather than later. "I do want to stay, but honestly, I'd rather him not see me," she admitted.

"Sounds good to me. My feet are killing me," Claire Ann grumbled. The girls were all still nodding in agreement when the music stopped and Clive's voice came through the sound system.

"Where's that Kylie Ryans at tonight? Come on up here, girl. We have a surprise for you," he boomed.

I'm right here, Kylie thought. *Trying my damnedest to disa-freaking-pear.*

chapter THIRTY SIX

KYLIE couldn't help but smile at the cat calls and whistles that followed her to the stage, though she'd have felt much more comfortable in her boots instead of these damn stilettos. And if she looked to her left, her heart would break wide open for everyone to see.

She stood in the glare of the spotlight, shaking her head as the entire bar broke into an off key drunken version of *Happy Birthday*. Tonya and a new waitress Kylie didn't know wheeled out a cart with a gorgeous and entirely too huge bright pink birthday cake in the shape of a guitar. She couldn't help but grin as she blew out the candles, but the wish that flew uninvited into her mind almost made her frown.

When they'd finished, Clive clamped a big hand onto her shoulder. "Since we sang to you, we're kinda hopin' you're gonna sing a few for us," he told her with a wink at the audience.

Kylie stared at Clive because she knew there was only one person she'd see if she looked into the crowd. Well, two people.

"Clive Hodges, ladies and gentlemen. He will even make you work on your birthday, even if you don't actually work here anymore," she said into the mic.

Laughter filled the bar. And then she did find his face because he was the only one not smiling. He looked like he might be in pain. Well, good. That made two of them.

Kylie spoke quietly to the band and then turned back to the audience as she strapped on a guitar Andy from the house band handed her.

"Typically I do covers since I'm still unsigned and don't have an album of my own out yet, but this place is special to me. I'm going to sing a song I wrote on coffee and no sleep so if it doesn't make sense, well then you can all Tweet that I've lost my mind." More laughter. "Just baring my soul here people. Laugh it up," she said with a wink. "This is called *Heartbreak Town*. I hope you like it."

Kylie strummed a few chords and Andy followed. God. She had lost her mind. She was about to sing the song she'd written about Trace. And it was going to be obvious as hell. Thank goodness she'd made it a fast one at least. But the slow parts at the beginning and end were going to feel like daggers scraping her raw.

My friends keep sayin' I need to let you go. Don't know how I'm 'sposed to do that though when it seems like, you're everywhere, in this heartbreak town. Even though I know it's wrong, you turned my life into a country song and I keep playin' it, on repeat.

When the drums kicked in and the tempo tripled, Kylie let herself go, unleashing the chorus at the top of her lungs. *Wish I could pack up and move away, but this emptiness is here to stay. There's no gettin' out, gettin' out, of this heartbreak town. Promises were made and broken so fast, I don't know how, but the pain still lasts and I'm stuck here, walkin' round this heartbreak town.*

Her subconscious warned her not to look at him. But her eyes weren't listening.

One day I know there'll be no more tears to cry and I'll have to get on with my life, when all that's left are memories of, ashes from a night that burned. But for now I carry them around, walkin' alone in this heartbreak town.

She made it through the next few lyrics because she was so into the song she nearly forgot where she was. And where he was. Until the background music faded as she sang one more chorus. Then the last few lines she sang slowly, a capella. *My friends keep sayin' I need to let you go. Don't know how I'm 'sposed to do that though when it seems like you're everywhere in this heartbreak town…*

Silence and blood rushing in her ears filled the seconds after she'd finished. Trace held her captive, locked in his stare and she couldn't break free. Even when the audience went crazy, whooping and hollering like riled up animals and a slow smile spread across her face, she was still trapped in the fiery gaze that burned into her from below a mess of dark hair.

"Thank y'all," she said softly into the microphone. Her hands tingled and her legs were going numb. The combination of the rush of performing and Trace staring at her with an expression she couldn't decipher made her lightheaded.

"One more song! One more song!" some fool in the back began chanting. Within seconds it caught on and the audience, save for two people sitting in the middle of the bar, was on its feet demanding an encore.

One particular song was playing steadily in the back of her mind and had been since she'd seen Trace with Mia, but it would be pretty obvious that she was jealous if she sang it. So she wasn't going to. But then Mia Montgomery leaned over, snaked an arm around Trace's shoulders and whispered something into his ear. And he smiled, a grin fit for the devil. And now she had to sing it. Because it was either that, or punch the most recent American Idol in her perfect face.

"Alright, alright," she laughed into the mic. "One more, cause I love y'all so much. But after this one, I've got to get back to my friends." After the cheering and whistling died down, she spoke again. "Some guy once told me that I wasn't a nice girl, so I just want to let y'all know up front… he was right."

After leaning over to tell Andy the song, he smiled and shook his head but began playing. Just as she sank her teeth into Carrie Underwood's *Good Girl* she saw surprise and maybe hurt ripple across Trace's face. No way was she staying up on this stage.

Kylie pulled the mic free and sang the lyrics aimed at Mia Montgomery while sauntering all over the bar. She even hopped up on the actual mahogany bar and placed a chaste kiss on Derek the hot bartender's cheek. Or maybe it was Devon. Whichever.

When she was finished, she was too busy being accosted by fans to get another look at Trace and his date. By the time she made it back to her table, they were gone.

"I am officially a fan," Carmen said, grinning. "Damn, Kylie. I knew you could sing but I don't think anyone in Pride knew you had that in you."

"I did," Lulu chirped.

"Thanks," Kylie said quietly. Rae and Claire Ann were nowhere to be seen. Her stomach and heart flipped and turned in what felt like an attempt to switch places. "Think Trace's sisters are mad at me?" she asked as she grabbed her bottle of water.

"Who cares," Carmen answered.

"I doubt it," Lulu told her. "Trace got up after you kissed the smokin' hot bartender and they followed that chick he brought out after him. Said they wanted to say goodbye."

"Ah."

"You want to get out of here? Get something greasy to go and put another notch in that bucket of mint chocolate chip before we hit the airport?"

Damn Lulu for being able to read her like a book. "Yeah, I really do," Kylie answered honestly. "Think he'll ever stop having this effect on me?" she asked too low for Carmen to hear.

"I don't know." Her friend gave her a small smile. "But it looked like you had a pretty serious effect on him, too, if that helps any."

Kylie shrugged. It didn't.

After her to-go order of loaded cheese fries came up, she told Clive and Tonya goodnight and headed out of the bar with her two remaining friends. She sucked in a deep breath of outside air as she pushed through the doors.

And ran smack into Trace, his sisters, and Mia Montgomery.

"Oh!" Kylie's mouth dropped open in a little *o* of surprise as she crashed into Trace, the hot bag of cheese fries smashing between them.

"Easy," Trace said, placing his hands on her shoulders to steady her.

"Yeah, I guess I was," she snapped, jerking out from under his grasp. Why was she so angry all of the sudden?

Dark hazel eyes widened, but he didn't say anything in response.

"We're heading back to Kylie's now," Lulu broke in. "Y'all comin'?" she asked in Rae and Claire Ann's direction.

"Um, we're gonna stay at Trace's tonight," Rae answered. "But thanks for letting us crash your party."

"Any time," Kylie told the girl, giving her a hug, cheese fries and all. "Thanks for coming," she whispered before they broke apart. "You too, Claire Ann," she told the older girl with a nod.

"It was fun, thanks," Claire Ann told her.

"You ready?" Lulu asked just as Trace had pinned Kylie in another of his intense glares.

"Um, yeah," she said, finally breaking free. If her stupid heart was going to pound like this every time he was around, she was going to have to seriously avoid him for totally legitimate health reasons. Carmen and Lulu flanked her on either side. Just as Claire Ann and Rae were doing to Trace. *The line's been drawn*, she thought sadly.

"Happy birthday, Kylie Lou," Trace said quietly, just as she was about to walk away. She saw Mia standing awkwardly behind him. Why did he have to bring her? He ruined everything. Kylie bit her lip to keep it from quivering and giving her pain away.

"Thanks," she whispered. Before either of them could say anything else, Kylie's phone rang. Her ringtone was Trace's song, *Waitin' for You to Call.* And she wanted to die right there on the sidewalk. It was Chaz calling.

"Um, I probably need to take this," she said, looking up at everyone around her. Trace nodded at his sisters and Mia and then they were gone.

"HOPE you're enjoying your birthday, Kylie, but I need you to meet me bright and early tomorrow at the studio so we can talk," her manager informed her.

Geez, what was with all the early morning meetings?

"Okay. I'm about to take my friends to the airport then head home to get some rest. See you at eight?" No need to mentioned the junk food fest they were about to have. She stuck her arm out to hail a cab but someone else snagged it before the girls could catch up to where it had stopped.

"Your session starts at eight. Come a few minutes early so we can chat."

Kylie said goodbye to her manager, and Lulu put her arm around her as they waited for another cab. "For what it's worth, he looked a hell of a lot more interested in you than the leggy brunette."

Kylie just shrugged. He tried to talk to her this morning and she'd messed it up. And then he'd moved on at breakneck speed. It hurt. Damn, did it hurt. But she had made a promise to her daddy and vowed to keep it. So she would. Music came first. Trace Corbin obviously didn't want anything more from her anyways. Somehow, some way, she'd figure out the necessary procedure for extracting her memories of Trace from her passion for music. She had a feeling she might need habit-forming narcotics afterwards.

After seeing Lulu and Carmen off to the airport a few hours later, Kylie returned home feeling…lonely. And confused. What the hell had happened with Trace tonight? Why had he brought Mia Montgomery to her party? Surely he had enough sense to know that would be hurtful. Kicking off her heels and slipping out of her dress, she flopped down on her bed. Trying to figure out why Trace Corbin did anything was exhausting.

KYLIE walked into Bluebird Studios with her head held high and battling the urge to fidget with everything she was worth. Her manager was going to tell her one of two things. Either she'd been chosen to fill the available space on The Random Road Trip tour or she hadn't.

If the answer was no, she'd have to find a way to keep money coming in so she'd have enough to cover the additional studio time she'd need to record a demo. She didn't regret giving the extra money she'd had to Tonya, but she was worried about how slowly things were moving now. If the answer today was no, Chaz had some contacts at local venues and had mentioned getting her a few gigs soon. She used this information to comfort herself as the pretty redhead at the front desk gave her directions to Studio D, where she was recording today.

The painful fact that staying in Nashville would probably mean running in to him nagged at her as she made her way through the halls. Not just him—him and his new girlfriend—and God, Kylie really didn't know if her heart could take much more of that. Pushing the door open, she was greeted by a plush lounge area next to a high tech sound booth. Chaz and two other guys stood in the lounge area and stopped their conversation when she entered.

"There she is. Kylie Ryans, this is Brent Cursh and Matt Lane. They're the studio sound guys who'll be helping us out today." Chaz nodded to each of them as he spoke.

The skinny redhead didn't look to be much older than she was, but the heavy set man with a receding hair line and kind eyes looked about Clive's age.

Kylie smiled at them both, grateful to have people willing to help her. This side of making music she had no clue about. "Morning. Nice to meet y'all."

After they all shook hands and exchanged pleasantries, the two sound guys excused themselves so she and Chaz could speak privately. She wished she'd had the foresight to bring everyone coffee to show her gratitude. But her body was already amped up and trembling with anticipation as it was. Kylie's nerves were getting the best of her and she hoped the guys hadn't noticed her sweaty palms.

"Chaz, I'm dying here."

"Okay, so are you ready for this?" His eyes were bright behind his rectangular frames. She tried to read his expression to determine if it was good news or bad news.

"Um, I think so."

"So at first, I got a firm no. Not because they didn't like you—they did. But with the negative publicity from your stepmom's craziness and the situation with Trace, they were going to go with a different girl."

Disappointment tugged at Kylie's heart but she didn't interrupt.

"So I asked them what could change the no into a yes. A friend of mine who happens to be engaged to a Vitamin Water exec said that if you had a hit single, or even a remotely popular single out, then they would've chosen you."

"But I don't," Kylie reminded him quietly.

"Right, not yet. But I remembered you mentioning that you and Trace had written a song together on the road the night we met, and I passed that information along to my friend. She said that just having recorded a song with Trace Corbin would be enough to put you in front of the other chick, even if the song isn't getting radio play yet. Soo...long story short, we get our asses in gear and record your vocals for that song you wrote. Then I'll talk to Trace's people and we'll get his vocals and ta da—off on tour you go!"

Oh this was bad. This was very bad. The walls of Kylie's world softened and threatened to cave in on her. "Um, Chaz? I can't record that song." She could barely remember even telling him about it that night in South Carolina. But she had been trying to impress him so he'd take her on as a client.

"Look Kylie, I'm not blind. Or deaf. I hear things. I know you and Mr. Corbin had a little fling on the road and that it might be difficult. But it's not like you have to marry him. You just have to—"

"No, Chaz. I mean I *can't*. As in legally, I can't. Because I signed papers yesterday saying that I wouldn't." Jesus. Yesterday had been the longest damn day of her life.

For a moment, Kylie worried her apparently healthy thirty-three year old manager was having a heart attack. His blue eyes bulged from behind his glasses and his face turned a deep shade of crimson.

"You did what? When?" His voice was strained and he began shaking his head as if he didn't believe her.

"Yesterday morning. I met Pauly Garrett for breakfast and signed several papers saying I relinquished all my rights to the song Trace and I wrote and that I wouldn't record it. With anyone. Ever."

Her manager's eyes went wide as he took a step back. "Why the fuck would you do that? Without even talking to me? Why did you even ask me to be your manager if you were just going to do whatever the hell you wanted anyways?" Chaz was standing over her, raining angry questions that she couldn't answer.

"I'm sorry, Chaz. Listen—"

"No, Kylie. *You* listen. I busted my ass to negotiate this deal for you, called in favors and pulled strings with people who I now owe, so that you could go on this tour in hopes that it would help you land an agent and a lucrative record deal. And you went behind my fucking back and signed some bullshit papers that you probably didn't even read or get a copy of."

Her head dropped in shame because he was right, and so he wouldn't see the tears filling her eyes. How could she have been so stupid? This was exactly what Trace had been warning her about all along.

"You have got to be kidding me." Her manager huffed out a loud breath. "Do you even want to do this?"

"Yes, of course I do. It's what I've always dreamed of." But her voice lacked conviction. She didn't know what had happened to her, to that girl she once was who carried her guitar everywhere, sacrificed everything for music, and wouldn't have let her stupid heart get in the way of her one shot at her dream. Trace had told her. Pauly had told her. Hell, even Tonya had said, "You'll never get anywhere in this business if you keep letting your emotions make all of your decisions." They were all right. And she was too damn headstrong to listen, too busy telling Trace how it was to hear what was he was trying to warn her about.

Her manager shook his head. "I'm done here. There are a thousand other girls who would've loved to be in your shoes."

Kylie choked back a sob. Not a sad one—an angry one. Directed at herself. "You mean you're done helping me with the Vitamin Water people? Surely there will be other tours and maybe we can just focus on recording and—"

"No, Ms. Ryans. I mean I'm *done.* As in, I don't need this shit. Find yourself another manager. And don't screw him over when he tries to help you."

So this is what it feels like to lose everything. Again.

"Chaz, wait. Please, just tell me what I can do." She barely resisted the urge to reach out and grab him, throw herself at his feet like a child and beg him not to go. Her career couldn't be over before it had even begun. It just couldn't.

Turning to face her, he took a deep breath before speaking. "Honestly, the only thing I can think of is calling Mr. Corbin and his manger and finding out if they've given those contracts to the label yet. If they have, you're pretty much screwed because it's out of their hands. But if they haven't, maybe you can convince them to tear them up and let you record the song with him. That's all I've got."

Okay, well, that might work. At least he had a plan. "Okay, so will you do that?"

"Will I do what?" he asked, his brow wrinkling as he spoke.

"Call Tra, er, Mr. Corbin and ask him."

Kylie watched as her manager, if he was still in fact her manager, pressed his fingers behind his glasses to rub his eyes and then his temples. "No, I won't. You signed those papers. You dug this hole for yourself. Now you can pull yourself out of it. If and only if they agree to do this will I consider still being your manager. But so help me, Kylie, if you ever pull some shit like this on me again, not only will we be done, I'll tell everyone I know to steer clear of your unbalanced ass."

"Got it," she nodded. "Thank you. And for what it's worth…I'm sorry."

For a moment, the man just stared at her as if trying to make up his mind about something. Then he sighed and turned away from her, exiting the studio and leaving her alone.

Standing there wallowing in her own shame, Kylie jumped when the door opened. The young red-haired guy poked his head in. "You ready, Ms. Ryans?"

"Um, I think I might need to reschedule."

"Hi Pauly. It's me," she said into the phone as she sat in her empty apartment. A few new pieces of furniture that she now regretting buying had just been delivered, and if Pauly had already given those documents to the label, she was going to have to return every bit of it.

"Kylie," he clipped. "What can I do for you?"

"Um, I have a question actually."

The manager sighed, almost as if he knew what was coming. "Shoot."

"So Chaz was pretty pissed about me signing those papers. Well, the ones about the song." He probably didn't give two shits about the NDA, though that was the one that hurt her the most.

"Yeah, I imagine he would be. I told you not to just go signing things without him and or a lawyer present. For all you knew, you could've been signing away every song you ever recorded."

Jesus. She hadn't even thought of that. "Is that how it is, Pauly? Nobody really cares about anybody? Everybody's just out to screw each other?" Literally, in her case. "Because if I'd known I was signing my whole damn career away, I would've listened." Lord did she hate herself for not listening. She didn't listen to Trace's advice about her career and she sure didn't listen when he told her he didn't do relationships. Or at least her heart didn't listen. She swallowed the lump forming in her throat. This was about business. She had to remind herself to keep her stupid deaf heart out of it.

Another big sigh from the man on the other end. "Look, kid. No one is out to get you. I work for Trace—I do what I have to with his best interests in mind. I don't always like it and I don't always agree with it. Is that what you called to ask me?"

She could practically see him checking his watch.

"No, it's not. I called to see if you still had those contracts or if you'd already given them to the label."

In the seconds that passed before he answered, Kylie crossed her fingers, said a silent prayer, and wished she had something to burn to the gods of music.

"To be honest, I'm not sure if the label has them or not. I passed them along to Trace. He may still have them."

Her chest ached to breathe a sigh of relief, but she couldn't. Not yet. "So um, any idea where I might find him?"

"Hold on," she heard him say, but she was pretty sure he was talking to someone in person and not her. "Yeah, I think he's in Macon for a few days. You may want to call out there and check first. But if he's already handed the contracts over, then there won't be much he can do for you either."

"I understand. Thanks for your time, Pauly."

"Take care, kid."

She ended the call and scrolled through her phone for Rae's number. She might've found it amusing that she didn't even have Trace's number if it didn't hurt so much. Just as she was about to hit the call button on the screen, an incoming call interrupted her. She didn't recognize it, but it had an Oklahoma area code. Maybe Lulu had gotten a new phone.

"Hello?"

"Mrs. Ryans?" an unfamiliar male voice said. Kylie's skin prickled. For a moment she thought it might be a reporter calling to confirm whatever crazy bullshit Darla was spouting now.

"This is Miss Ryans. Kylie Ryans," she told him, placing her finger over the red end button.

"My apologies, Miss Ryans. My name is Kevin Ryder and I'm with with Eternal Marble Memories. I received your online payment this morning and I was calling to schedule an appointment for designing Mr. Ryans' headstone."

Kylie's thoughts scattered. She snagged the closest one because it made the most sense.

"There must be some mistake, Mr. Ryder. I didn't make an online payment, or any kind of payment for that matter." And there was no way in hell Darla would have paid for her dad's tombstone and put Kylie's name as the contact. Eternal Marble Memories was one of the most expensive companies she'd found when researching places to purchase a headstone for her dad. They specialized in custom monuments and the cheapest thing they had was several thousand dollars more than Kylie could afford.

She heard what sounded like the clicking of a keyboard. "Well, someone obviously wanted Robert Kyle Ryans to have the best that money could buy, because I have a receipt here for five thousand dollars along with strict instructions to place anything over that amount on the credit card I have on file."

"Can you give me the name on the credit card you have on file?" she asked, even though she was pretty sure she knew exactly whose name was on that card. Or she had a good guess at least.

"Um, hang on just a sec—here it is. Looks like the card we charged the payment to belongs to a Tracey M. Corbin."

Kylie clutched the phone so hard her nails nearly dented the protective cover.

"Miss Ryans, are you still there?"

Was she?

"Yeah. Yes, sir. Um, about the appointment. I'm not in Oklahoma." *You will be soon if Trace has already submitted those documents to Capital.* Her snarky subconscious hinted at what she was already in the process of figuring out. Like the overpayment from the tour, this was Trace's way of relieving his guilt. Because of course he would've already turned in those contracts. Why else would Pauly have made such a big deal about getting them signed so quickly?

"That's not a problem, Miss Ryans."

Kylie couldn't think straight. Hell yes it was a problem—the one thing she had plenty of was problems.

"We have an online gallery to choose from. You can place your order online or by phone at your convenience." Right, okay. *Focus, Kylie.*

"Um, okay, got it. Thank you."

Mr. Ryder gave Kylie the website and phone number she needed and thanked her for her business. Kylie mumbled something she hoped was intelligible. Her hands shook as she sat the phone down on her coffee table. Pulling her knees to her chest, she tried to fight off the panic attack that was speeding towards her. If Trace did this, he did it out of guilt. Because he'd probably turned in those contracts, and he knew what she'd been giving up even if she didn't realize it until Chaz went berserk.

She had to talk to Trace, had to beg, plead, or whatever else was necessary, to get him to get those papers back. Swallowing her pride, she knew it was time to admit that he was right about this being a business. She had to get her shit together and get over her heartbreak so they could record this song together. *Just get through this and then you can go back out on the road and forget him*. Except she would never really be able to forget him. But that was a crisis for another day.

chapter THIRTY NINE

"CLAIRE Ann, it has to be you," she pleaded. "He knows Rae will lie for me and he'll suspect something."

"Kylie, are you sure this is the right thing to do? You know how he feels about surprises." The tone of her voice made it clear she was less than excited to be a part of Kylie's plan. But after what had happened this morning, there was no way Kylie was going to back out now.

"Claire Ann, I got a call from a place called Eternal Marble Memories today. Trace paid for my dad's headstone to surprise me. We have… unfinished business." That was putting it mildly. "I really need to see him. Please, will you help me?"

A sigh came from the other end of the line and couldn't help but smile into the phone. "What do I have to do?"

After she'd explained her plan, she held her breath, waiting for Claire Ann's response.

"You owe me," Trace's older sister told her.

"I know."

SEVERAL hours later, Kylie struggled to stay awake on Trace's couch in his mini studio. She was glad to see that at some point he'd finished the wiring in the recording room because they were going to need it.

When she heard a key turning in the lock she jumped and sat up on the couch, faced the door, and waited. Her whole body tingled nearly to the point of twitching in anticipation. *Please do not let him have filed those contracts.* Her heart had a plea of its own. *Please let him be alone and let him be happy to see me.*

The man who stepped through the doorway was carrying a baseball bat. Oh hell.

"Trace?" she asked timidly, unable to see clearly in the dark. It was nearly eleven o'clock.

"Kylie?" he asked, lowering the bat. Thank God.

"Hey."

He flicked on a lamp and she could see that he was exhausted. His five o'clock shadow was well on into its evening, his clothes were wrinkled to hell and back, and his hair was a mess.

"Rough night?" she asked.

"Rough life," Trace answered, stepping slowly towards her.

"Yeah, same here," she said softly.

"Not that I'm not happy to see you, but can I ask what you're doing here?"

"You know I always have to have the last word," she said, smiling up at him.

He arched an eyebrow but said nothing.

"I told you when I was out of a job you'd come home to find me crashed out on this couch."

Trace cleared his throat. "I guess I didn't realize you were serious."

"Yeah, well, I wasn't at the time."

He lowered himself onto the loveseat across from her. "Wait, what do you mean you're out of a job? I heard you were doing some Flavored Water tour."

"Vitamin Water," she corrected. "And I was. Or I am. At least, I hope I am. That's kind of why I'm here."

Trace's dark brows dipped as he crossed his arms over his chest. "I'm not following."

"Yeah, I'm not doing a very good job of explaining." Kylie composed herself the best she could and continued. "You were right about…some things. I should've listened." Her mouth went dry. She hadn't expected it to be this hard. Songs she could write all day. Telling people off when they were acting like asses, no problem. But admitting she was wrong and had royally screwed up sucked. Trying to do it in the presence of the man who smelled like heaven and happened to be sexy as hell? Damn near impossible.

"Which *things* would you be referring to, specifically?" Trace asked, eyeing her with interest and uncrossing his arms.

Breathe, Kylie. Just say what you came to say. "My getting signed to The Random Road Trip Tour was contingent upon me having a single out, and there really isn't time to make that happen. But Chaz pulled some strings and the people in charge of booking for the tour said it would be enough if I had at least recorded a song with you, specifically the one that we wrote together. The one I signed away all rights to without so much as mentioning it to my manager."

Tears began to gather behind her eyes as she realized what a truly stupid and selfish thing she had done by letting her emotions get the best of her. "I don't have an agent yet, so Chaz was working really hard to help me and I…screwed up." Kylie choked down the sob trying to escape before it could break free.

Trace raked a hand roughly over his stubbled jaw. His probing glare implored her to keep talking. "I'm guessing since you paid for my father's headstone, which I'd like to pay you back for by the way, that you've already given the papers I signed to the label. Look, I know you don't owe me any favors—"

"Whoa, hold up a sec. Please tell me what in the ever-loving fuck my paying for your dad's headstone has to do with my giving those papers to the label?" Trace's voice was edged with something that sounded an awful lot like anger.

"I may have done some stupid stuff since you've known me, Trace, but I am actually not a complete idiot. You overpaid me for the tour because you felt guilty for sleeping with me. You sent a memorial company entirely too much money for my dad's headstone because you felt bad for submitting the paperwork that ensured I wouldn't be able to record our song. Surely you knew that would be damaging to me in some way. Even Pauly practically chewed me out for signing them without reading them or consulting Chaz first." And yet, she'd done it anyways.

Trace leaned forward and Kylie's head reeled from the closeness. His cologne surrounded her, and the fact that she didn't smell liquor on him made her wonder where he'd been all night. "You know, for a smart girl, you sure do say some dumb shit sometimes."

Kylie flinched at the harsh words.

"First," he began, sticking up his index finger. "You were not overpaid for the tour. You were given the exact amount agreed upon, which you would know if you'd bothered to Read. The. Damned. Contract." He paused and shook his head. "Second," he continued, adding another finger to the count, "I sure as hell don't feel guilty for sleeping with you. I feel bad about the way things went down, yes, but not for anything other than that. Unless you tell me right now, to my face, that you regret it, I will never feel anything but sheer joy about what happened that night." Trace leaned back and waited for her to say it. But she couldn't because she didn't. She couldn't keep still under the intensity of his stare either, so she squirmed and looked away. He continued with his counting. "And third, I paid for the headstone because I wanted to. Because I owe something to the man who raised the only woman I've ever known who can put me in my place. In fact, I owe him a hell of a lot more than that."

Just like that, the delicate layer left protecting Kylie's heart began to shatter, splintering and cracking like ice over a flame. Her dad would've liked Trace. A lot, probably. But they would never meet.

"Trace." A sob escaped her throat, so Kylie clamped her mouth shut and put her hand over it. There was so much, too much, she wanted to say. To ask, to understand. She couldn't let it all out at once or it would crush them both.

The beautiful man across from her sighed and reached out to touch her cheek. "Kylie, you were right about a lot of things. But so was I. And we were both wrong about a few things, too."

"You brought that girl to my party," she choked out. Because underneath it all, that was bothering her the most.

"So you could meet her and see that there was nothing going on between us. She was excited to meet you. She was a fan until you got all up in her face with that damned song. Well played, by the way."

"You called me a shitty life choice." She tried to lower her head, but his fingers pressed her chin upward, forcing her to keep facing him.

"I called all the stupid-ass decisions I made that drew media attention to my family before I even met you shitty life choices. You just never stuck around to listen to my explanation."

Oh God. Kylie jerked back from his touch, pulling her knees up and lowering her face to meet them. "Never mind. Forget everything I said. I actually am a complete idiot," she mumbled without looking up.

"No you're not. You just feel first and think second. I love that about you actually. But sometimes it can get your cute little ass into trouble."

Her head snapped up at his words. "You kept saying no one cared, that it was just business, and I kept hearing *you* didn't care and it was just sex."

"Well…I do care. And if you think that was just sex, then I must've done something wrong."

"But Darla—"

"Fuck Darla."

Kylie snorted. "Half of Oklahoma already has."

"There's my girl." Trace chuckled and shook his head. "Look, she caught me off guard and I lost it a little. By the time I came to my senses and saw it for what it was, you were writing me off as a fling and I didn't know what to do about it. So I got drunk, because that's always been my fallback." Trace raked a hand through his hair. "And then we really screwed each other, and not in the hot, mind-blowingly amazing way like we did here. More like in the excruciatingly painful, break-each-other-into-a-million-pieces way. But I never wanted to hurt you, Kylie. Even if it was just fling for you, I'll never be sorry that we did what we did, and I'll never try to hurt your chances of having a career."

He'd thrown so much information at her that she wasn't sure what to respond to first. Instinct said feelings first. Act on feelings—kiss him, throw self at him. Repeat. *Now.* But she was learning. She had to stop feeling first and thinking second. That was what had gotten her into this mess to begin with. Handle the business first, heart second.

She wiped away a tear that was in the process of escaping onto her cheek. "If you really don't want to hurt me, talk to the label. Convince them to tear up the contracts and let us record the song together so that I can get on this tour and get my manager back. Please."

It was the wrong thing to respond to first. Kylie could tell by the way his bright eyes went dim and the obvious effort it took for him to smile at her.

"I, um, still have the papers. I didn't give them to anyone. And even if I had, they don't say what you think they do." Trace stood and walked over to a table with several folders on it. He grabbed one and came back to her with it extended.

She took the folder and opened it, relief washing over her when she recognized her signature.

"I knew you wouldn't read them, hothead that you are. After you signed them and Pauly gave them to me, I had to admit to myself how low it was for me to have lost it on you for lying and then turned around and tricked you into signing something saying you'd record with me. It was shitty, I know, but I just couldn't forget the way it felt that night. With you. Here. Writing and knowing how great we could be together." He cleared his throat. They'd done a lot more than just writing. "I've never been a relationship kind of man. But being with you here made me want to try." Trace huffed out a huge breath as if he'd been carrying the burden of those words for far too long.

There was so much unfiltered honesty in his words that she was high on it. So much so that it made her lightheaded. "Wait, these say that I'll record the song with you? Pauly said—"

"Pauly lied…for me. He works for me, remember?"

So that was why he'd run out of the diner like his ass was on fire. Kylie couldn't help but grin. "You know, now that I think about it, he's not that great of a liar. He tried his damnedest to get me to read these."

"Not everyone can be as good at it as you and me." Trace laughed but it was empty laughter. She wondered if it was because he thought this was all she came for.

"The morning of my birthday, you left before…" she took a deep breath, hoping she'd suck in some of his courage along with it.

"Before?" Trace prompted, lowering himself back onto the couch across from her.

"Before I could tell you that I care about you, too." As soon as the words were out of her mouth, Trace went completely still. For a full minute he stared long and hard at her. Kylie sat up straight and braced herself for whatever was coming.

"I'm seeing someone," he said quietly.

Her shoulders sagged and she fought with everything she had to keep the corners of her mouth from turning down. Why did she have to be so damn stupid? Mia Montgomery. He was seeing her now. His declaration stole the air from her lungs so she inhaled deeply before speaking.

"Okay," Kylie said swallowing and nodding. This was it. She'd given it everything she had. And it was just over. Men like Trace didn't sit around and wait for girls like her to figure out what they wanted. She stifled a shiver as reality crashed cold and hard all over her. "Well, I'm happy for you," she choked out. The walls closed in and she just wanted to get the hell out of there. Her mind began plotting the best escape route. *Hold on a damn minute, hothead*, she scolded herself. "We can still record the song, right? As friends?"

"About my drinking," Trace added slowly. "I don't want to be my father, so I've been talking to an addiction specialist that's a friend of Pauly's. And you were right. Claire Ann, Rae, and you, Kylie—you all deserve better."

She waited for the punch line but he didn't say anything else. "So you are or you aren't dating Mia Montgomery?" she asked, side-eying him with a glare.

"No, I'm not dating anyone. But see how it feels to be lied to and toyed with?" he laughed. And the fist gripping Kylie's heart finally let go. So she chucked a square throw pillow at his head.

"You are not a nice boy," she said pointing a finger at him.

"Never said I was," he told her as he leaned in dangerously close. Kylie breathed in the clean familiar scent of cologne and Trace.

"No more lies," she mumbled against his lips as they brushed hers.

"Uh huh," Trace murmured against hers before leaning back, denying her the kiss she wanted more than air. "So you're telling me Claire Ann really thinks someone broke in here?"

"No. She knows someone did…because I told her I was going to." Kylie laughed and pulled him back to her. "Wait, I'm doing it again. Feeling first and thinking second. There's no time for kissing! We have a song to record because, if Chaz can forgive me and the Vitamin Water people agree, I'm leaving for my tour Friday morning."

"I feel so cheap and used." He laughed again, his real laugh, the deep throaty one that sent chills racing up her spine and filled her with warmth all at once. It was the most beautiful sound she'd ever heard. It filled her with the same intoxicating mixture of contentment and excitement that hearing her dad play guitar always had.

"Good, I plan to use you up every chance I get," she teased just before placing a lingering kiss firmly on his lips.

"This is really what you want then? To be with a burned out has-been even though you're going on tour and about to become a huge star?" His hands slid up the sides of her shirt as he pulled her into his lap.

"More than anything," she told him, resting her forehead on his. And it was the truth.

"Good, because I wasn't going to let you leave this room if you said no, and there is *always* time for kissing." He twisted a hand into her hair and claimed her mouth with the deepest kiss of her life. When his warm, wet tongue lashed against hers, Kylie whimpered and bit down gently on his bottom lip.

Trace pulled back from their kiss again just as she was losing herself in it completely. "Wait, now we need to talk about something really important."

"What?" She groaned, praying this wasn't going to be something that ruined the euphoric high about to carry her away.

"About those sexy shirt-earning mechanical bull riding skills of yours…"

"Down, boy," Kylie told him, brushing her nose playfully against his and kissing him once more as her heart swelled with happiness. "We have a song to record."

Kylie Ryans – Real Life Cinderella Story or Just Another Girl with SDI (Serious Daddy Issues)?

By Tammy Paxton

Anyone who hasn't heard that Nashville newcomer Kylie Ryans and fledgling superstar Trace Corbin did more on that tour bus than sleep must have been living under a rock. But while social media comments indicate that fans are pretty equally divided, torn when it comes to the Oklahoma native's country music star status (starlet or harlot—be honest, how did you vote?) as well as her intentions.

"Kylie would do anything for fame," her estranged stepmother proclaims to anyone who will listen. "She's developed a nasty habit of seducing older men to get what she wants."

While an interview with Ms. Ryans' high school music teacher resulted in a much more heartfelt story.

"Kylie is a tough girl who learned early on that she had a gift for music and that she could use that gift to cope with difficult situations in her life, such as losing her father unexpectedly less than a year ago," Dan Molarity tells *Country Weekly*.

Though both Corbin and Ryans are keeping quiet about their relationship status and have yet to make it Facebook official, there's no denying that Ryans rode in on the superstar's coattails, joining his tour after being discovered waitressing at the renowned Rum Room. Or maybe she was dragged in on them since Corbin's career has taken a noticeable dive as of late.

Rumors about Capital Letter Records possibly dropping the once platinum album-selling artist have plagued him steadily for the past year. So perhaps this new romance is mutually beneficial for both artists and the media attention will result in higher album sales and concert attendance. Or maybe fans will catch on that they're being played by the publicity machine and boycott both artists altogether.

Relationship status confirmation aside, Corbin, a well-known lover of attractive women and hard liquor, has definitely taken an interest in the previously unheard of Ryans. Reports have surfaced that he even took the stunning young blonde home to Macon to meet his family and friends. Which leaves some of us wondering if Corbin has been using, "Hey, there's a spot open on my tour," as a pick-up line or if Ryans in the real deal.

Nineteen-year-old Ryans recently hired publicist Cora Loughlin, (smart move, kid) who only commented so far as to say, "Kylie went through a difficult period after losing her father where she found herself with nothing to lean on other than her musical talent, which she immediately put to good use."

Ryans was recently asked to join Vitamin Water's *Random Road Trip* tour even though she has yet to commit to a label while Corbin is reportedly in talks to set dates for his *No Apologies* tour. The only way to determine whether or not Ryans has the chops to make it in Nashville is to see her perform, and once you do, you'll likely agree that she's more than a flash in the pan. However, the question remains: is there a real romance brewing between Corbin and Ryans or is this just a case of a young woman working out her daddy issues with a more than willing participant? Only time will tell. Well, time and maybe Twitter.

–TAMMY PAXTON

ONE

"HAVE you seen it?" Kylie screeched at her boyfriend via Skype.

"Yeah, Kylie Lou, I saw it," his pixelated image told her. "But I mean, so what? We knew they would talk." Trace shrugged his shoulders and glanced down at what Kylie knew was probably his iPhone in his hand.

"She said I had 'daddy issues,' Trace, like I'm using you or something, and the woman talked to freaking Darla of all people." Kylie leaned back in the tight booth on the bus, wishing she could reach out and let him put his arms around her. But she couldn't, so she folded her arms across her chest, knowing it wasn't attractive to pout but unable to help herself.

"Babe, it's not as bad as you think." He looked up and his warm hazel eyes stared into hers. "Actually, Tammy did a decent job of presenting both sides and she was honest for the most part. You know how it looks. There's not a whole lot about us that makes sense."

Ouch, she thought to herself as she flinched back from his comment. "Oh-kay. So you want to just forget the whole thing now? Save ourselves the trouble of figuring out what everyone else obviously already knows?" *Please say no.*

"Easy, hothead," her boyfriend said with a grin. "If one little article sends you running for the hills, I'm not sure I believe you're committed to this long-distance dating thing."

Kylie bit her lip to hold in the smile his words elicited. "You know I am, but my God, why is any of this anyone's business?" She still couldn't figure out why people cared what she did or what she ate for breakfast or whatever. No one back home in Pride, Oklahoma, had ever paid any attention to her, online or otherwise. Now she had a hit single and two hundred thousand people "following" her on Twitter.

"You remember that day on the bus, the day you met Cora?" Trace asked, as he snuck another glance at his phone.

"Yeah, and speaking of Cora, I've been meaning to ask—"

"No, we didn't," Trace cut her off, shaking his head. "Focus, Kylie. Remember what I said about having a thick skin?"

"Yeah, superhuman thick. I remember," she told him, leaning closer towards the MacBook screen. "I thought you were an ass but I was actually listening, believe it or not."

"Well, now you know I'm an ass. But I'm glad you were listening because this is what I was talking about. Don't stress about *what* they say Just be glad they're talking about you, period. Look at it as free publicity."

"Trace—" she began to argue but her own phone buzzed on the table next to the computer. She glanced at the screen. A handsome face behind rectangular black frames appeared. "Um, it's Chaz."

"Yeah, hey, I gotta get off here anyways. I have a meeting in a few minutes with Pauly and the band about the tour. Mike says hi by the way." At the mention of his flirty bass player, Trace rolled his eyes but kept going. "Don't stress. You look beautiful today. Miss you, babe," he said in a rush.

"Miss you, too." And then he was gone. Kylie closed the computer and touched the accept button on her screen.

"Hey there most awesomest, hardest working, handsomest manager ever," she greeted her caller.

"Good morning, gorgeous," he responded. "So, is Tammy Paxton a bitch or what?"

Kylie's gaze fell on the copy of *Country Weekly* lying open to her article on the table in front of her.

"Ugh, I know, right? Trace didn't think it was a big deal but the daddy issues thing was low."

"Yeah it was," her manager agreed enthusiastically. *See, he gets it.* Kylie was extremely glad that he was still her manager. She'd almost lost him when she let her emotions get the better of her. Trace hadn't nicknamed her "hothead" for nothing. "So I'm calling because I have news."

"About the cute guy from dinner last night? The one who flirted shamelessly with you over dessert and has already tweeted saying it was a pleasure to meet me and my manager?" she probed.

"No, that news is none of your business, my dear," her manager snapped with false snark.

"Yeah well, don't cut a country music album because then it will be everyone's business," Kylie informed him.

"'Kay, I'll check that off my list of things to do then. Listen, so I know you're probably enjoying having that big luxurious bus all to yourself right now but Lily Taite should be there within the hour so you can get going to Phoenix, and um…there's been a last minute change."

Lily Taite was Trace's younger sister Rae's age and had a rich daddy who'd paid for her album of whiny break up songs and probably her spot on the tour. She also dotted the Is in her name with pink hearts. Kylie wasn't all that enthusiastic about touring with her really, but it was Chaz's tone when he'd brought up the last minute change that made her nervous.

"What kind of change?"

"Lauryn McCray backed out…and rumors are spreading that she's pregnant."

Kylie was floored. Lauryn McCray was only a couple years older than her and had already written with some of country music's biggest stars. Kylie had been super excited to work with her. And now she was pregnant? She stared blankly at Chaz's image on her phone. He was clearly waiting for her to respond. "What?" Oh crap. That meant it was her and Princess Lily all alone. Awesome.

"Yeah, so the Vitamin Water people had a few backups on standby and they chose one. She should be there any minute." She opened her mouth to ask who but her manager rushed on. "I'm sorry I couldn't tell you sooner. I was on a conference call and just got their message about the situation."

Okay, well that was good news as far as she was concerned. So why did he seem so stressed out about it? "So who's going to be the third girl then?" she asked into the phone.

"I am," said an auburn-haired figure ascending the steps to the bus. "But just because I was added late doesn't mean you get top billing over me or anything."

"I'll call you back," Kylie murmured before ending the call.

"Mia Montgomery," the tall slender woman said, tossing Kylie a smirk as she held out her hand. "I don't think we've officially met."

For an extended Sneak Peek of Girl on Tour, visit the author's website at www.caiseyquinnwrites.com and sign up for News from Caisey Q.

I could write a whole other book about everyone I have to thank for making this one possible. I'll try to keep it brief. Warning: I suck at brief.

First and foremost, thank you God for the gift of words, for blessing me with a passion for reading and writing, and for the wonderful people who allow me to do both.

Thank you to my husband and daughter for putting up with me when I was living mostly in a world of fictional characters. For understanding, and for loving and supporting me always. Mama, thanks so much for all the voluntary babysitting so that I could write. And for believing in me when I didn't believe in myself. Thank you to my daddy in Heaven, for encouraging me to always finish what I start. I know you're watching over me. I hope you're proud.

My brother is the musical one in the family, bless his heart for helping his tone deaf sister with lyrics and explaining the mechanics of song writing. My in-laws are some pretty wonderful people who invested in me as an author and bought me my very first MacBook. Love y'all so much!

Thank you to Amber and Kevin Adams for not only answering my questions about Nashville and music, but for keeping my kiddo so I could write. Your friendship means more to me than you know.

From the bottom of my heart, thank you Emily Mah Tippetts. There aren't even words. Without you, there would be no book. Only a sad little word document saved on my computer with nowhere to go. Thank you for reading that hot mess of a first draft and taking a chance on some chick in Alabama. If I live to be one hundred, I'll never be able to repay you for the endless support and willingness to answer my every obsessive question. For letting me vent in emails that probably have a higher word count than this book. For working tirelessly on the cover design and embracing my brand of crazy. For reading my mind. For giving Kylie and Trace the ending they deserved. Thank you. A million times. Thank you. If I ever doubt God's love for me, I remember that He led me to you!

Much love, appreciation, and big "schmoopy" hugs to Diane Alberts, my other wonderful CP, who took the time to read Trace and Kylie's story and remind me that dialogue tags are our friends, even though she was right in the middle of moving. I'm also very fortunate that Mickey Reed offered to take me on at the last minute when I was in panic mode. You're a lifesaver and you're stuck with me now!

Even though they don't know it, I owe a huge thanks to some special people in Nashville. Thank you Blake Shelton and Miranda Lambert for being such an amazing example of what it means to be in love. Your story is the foundation on which this one is built. Thank you Luke Bryan for the wild ride of a concert that inspired the musical stylings of Trace Corbin. And for wearing such tight jeans. I basically stalked Jana Kramer at the start of her career, telling myself it was "research" for the progression of Kylie's. (If this book were a movie though, Jana would be Mia.) Thank you, Jana, for not pressing charges.

Lots of love and eternal gratitude to my number one fan, Tessa, who some of you know as @bookswinefood. Thank you for reading that first advance copy and for your enthusiasm as you bullied others into reading it! You're my soul sister!

Big crazy obnoxious shout out to my #countrygirls and #guttergirls on Twitter. Y'all are something else and I heart you crazy chicks more than you'll ever know!

And lastly and most importantly, thank you to my readers. This book is my heart in words. Thank you for the support, the Follows on Twitter, Likes on Facebook, your comments, reviews, and love. I love you right back, I really do. I feel like I should pay you to read my books instead of the other way around. Thank you for taking a chance on an unknown author. This is my dream come true and without you it wouldn't be possible. I hope you loved Trace and Kylie's story as much as I do and that you'll join them on the journey that is love on the road.

about the AUTHOR

Caisey Quinn lives in a suburb outside of Birmingham, Alabama with her husband, daughter, and other assorted animals. She wears cowgirl boots most of the time, even to church. Girl with Guitar is her first novel. Currently she is working on Girl on Tour, the second book in the Kylie Ryans series. She can be found online at www.caiseyquinnwrites.com.